Dark Vengeance

by

Dianne McCartney

The Elijah Black Trilogy, Book 1

Dark Vengeance

Cover Art by *Kim Mendoza*

The Wild Rose Press, Inc.
PO Box 708
Adams Basin, NY 14410-0708
Visit us at www.thewildrosepress.com

Publishing History
First Edition, 2022
Trade Paperback ISBN 978-1-5092-4038-8
Digital ISBN 978-1-5092-4039-5

The Elijah Black Trilogy, Book 1
Published in the United States of America

As Cassandra strolled past the crowd walking in the opposite direction, she beamed a smile and they reflexively smiled back without considering why. She was the perfect height, the perfect weight to be smiled at as she swung her purse in time to her cheerful, tapping steps.

They have no idea why I'm in such a fabulous mood. And I'm sure they'd be quite horrified if they did.

Her ill-gotten inheritance paid for her perfect teeth, glowing skin and the assortment of designer clothes that she wore. The sinfully expensive perfume that licked the air around her was a gift from a former lover who thought it would disguise his cheating heart.

How painfully naïve.

Unlike her, cheaters stank, the very scent of their inclinations permeating the souls of everyone around them. Cheaters and abusers deserved every ounce of pain they showered on others.

And more. So much more.

Praise for Dianne McCartney

Dark Vengeance won 2nd place in the 2020 OWFI Mainstream Novel Category under its working title, *Poetic Justice.*

Dedication

In loving memory of the late Det. Joe Tiroff, beloved friend and both homicide investigator and D.A. investigator in Fort Worth, Texas.

Acknowledgement

Thanks, as always, to my editor, the wonderful Ally Robertson, and the rest of the hard-working staff at The Wild Rose Press.

Other Wild Rose Press Titles by Dianne McCartney:

Just One Night
The Daughter of Death
The Road to Justice
Fear the Night

Chapter One

The butchered remains of Tanner King lay spread across the floor, the first digits of his recently removed fingers pointing at his massacred genitals. Detective Elijah Black raised a hand in greeting to the cops already on scene as he moved farther into the elegant hotel room to get a closer look.

Well, someone certainly wanted to make a point. Pulling on skintight vinyl gloves, he paused to scan the room before squatting beside the body. The victim's mouth contorted in a silent scream, his eyes bugged out from their sockets, making it quite certain he had been alive throughout the final indignities.

That couldn't have been much fun.

A billionaire, the handsome victim had a less-than-stellar reputation, according to the scant information provided. He was still mostly dressed, making the expensive tuxedo and shirt seem like a waste of money. His pants pooled around his knees, just enough to allow the killer access to the apparent goal.

Despite the gory scene, all he could think was that, due to this man's questionable character, there would be dozens of potential suspects waiting in the wings. The man-hours on this type of case would certainly pile up. Most murders demanded an outrageous amount of overtime.

Further investigation of the scene didn't yield

anything else of interest, so he stood back, allowing the newly arrived medical examiner, Dr. Stanford Hayes, to take a look. A person of high society always netted the best New York City had to offer. Stooping down to get a closer look, he said, "Well, I'd say he made someone very angry, indeed." After a preliminary check, he inserted the liver probe to read the temperature of the corpse. A few minutes later, he straightened, studying the device. "I estimate the time of death to be between nine and ten hours ago, Detective."

"Got it. Thanks." Plucking a pen from his pocket, he scrawled the information in his note pad.

"Let's turn him over." Together, they rolled him onto his stomach and found nothing beneath but clean carpet. They pushed him back to his former position.

"Do you have everything you need so I can release him?"

"Just let me check the pockets, Doc." He withdrew a slim, black leather wallet. Opening it revealed five hundred dollars cash in one-hundred-dollar bills, a few credit cards and his driver's license.

Elijah waved the crime scene technician forward to finish taking his pictures, including what he'd found. Two minutes later, he said, "Okay, Doc, I guess we're done."

"Fine. I'll let you know more as soon as possible." He allowed the attendants to remove the corpse. A few minutes later, they placed it in a black, zippered body bag and lifted it onto their gurney. They trundled their burden away, the doctor walking briskly at their heels.

Elijah glanced at his watch. It read a few minutes before 9 a.m., which put time of death between eleven and midnight last night. Casting around the hotel room,

Elijah noted it was unusually neat with nothing else appearing out of place. That observation and the fact King had still been wearing his ten-thousand-dollar watch and a diamond ring large enough to weight lift ruled out robbery as a motive. The focus of the attack being on his genitals would seem to suggest a woman.

But how many women would have the stomach to actually carry out this grisly crime?

He mulled that over as he worked his way around the room, staying out of the crime scene technicians' way with the ease of long practice.

The Montac's hyper hotel manager still hovered anxiously by the door, so he stopped to see what he wanted. The man's hands were shaking as he held out a sheet of paper and handed it to him. "My assistant just brought me this. The name of the woman who reserved the room is Cassandra Bell. My staff tell me she's a rather attractive blonde, tall and curvaceous."

"What time did she check in?"

"Mid-afternoon, yesterday."

"I assume she has already checked out?"

The man nodded like a bobble doll, his agitation creating an excess of energy. "Just after two a.m. this morning, according to our records. For obvious reasons, we were concerned about her welfare, but our night manager assures me that she seemed upbeat and didn't mention any problems."

It clearly hadn't occurred to him that she could be their killer. "Do you have your security people weeding out the relevant footage from your cameras?"

"Yes, sir...Detective. Our security guard just texted that the film is cued up on her exit. They are waiting for you downstairs."

Right on schedule, he heard the distinct tap-tap of heels approaching. Looking up, he smiled. "This is my partner, Detective Sanchez. She'll deal with your security staff and take care of evaluating anything on the feed."

The hotel manager hesitated at the appearance of his partner. Sanchez gave him a wink, taking a moment to band back her long, dark, wavy hair. At barely five-foot-five, everyone towered over her, but she moved as if powered by a battery pack. As always, her vibrant orange earrings swung in time to her constant motion. Stopping to glance inside the door, she let out a low whistle at the sight and shook her head in disbelief. "That's a hell of a way to say good morning." She led the manager away, talking like a radio disc jockey, pausing just long enough to breathe.

People often underestimated her, and that prejudice often worked in her favor. Street-savvy and bright, she was the perfect yin to his yang. She handled technology which frequently defeated him. His brain just didn't work that way. That enabled him to decipher crime scenes and deal with the brass. The past had proven he was far more diplomatic, and now she kept her lip zipped around the people who signed her paycheck.

Elijah stayed longer than normal, checking the scene, but time-honed instinct warned him of a difficult case. They'd found a single blonde hair, but other than that, the almost painfully clean room meant he didn't hold out much hope about the evidence that could be gleaned there.

King had been found by the maid whose name, according to the others, was Elena. Elijah went over to speak to her as she sat, shaking, on the bed in the empty room next door. Hispanic, in her mid-forties, she had a tear-stained face and a shocked expression. *Not a great start to anyone's day.*

He smiled at the female cop who'd stayed by the woman's side, , then turned to her. "Elena, my name is Detective Black. Are you feeling okay?"

"N-no, sir. I feel sick. Who would do such a violent thing?"

"That's what we hope to find out. Can you tell me what time you arrived at Mr. King's suite?"

She held up a clipboard, pointing. "At eight-twenty, sir. I have to log in my start time for each suite."

"Did you knock on the door?"

"Yes, sir. If no one answers, then we use the master key to enter unless there's a do not disturb sign on the doorknob."

He could tell she was nervous by her over-explaining as if he planned to give her a multiple-choice exam. "So, you opened the door and saw him lying on the floor. What did you do next?"

"I tried to scream, but no sound would come. My throat froze up, you know? So, anyway, I called the housekeeping manager and just said, 'I need help, please hurry' and gave her the room number."

"Did you go any further into the room than just standing in the doorway? It's okay if you did. We just have to know, so we can take your fingerprints and rule them out."

She shook her head vehemently, tousling her hair. "No, sir." Lifting a gold cross from the chain around her neck, she said, "I prayed for his soul and waited."

"Okay, good. How long did it take before your

supervisor showed up?"

Scrunching her face in thought, she said, "Four or five minutes. She had to run to catch the elevator and she was working down on the main floor."

"And what did she do when she arrived?"

"Her eyes bugged out when she saw him, but she didn't scream. She just pulled me outside. She closed the door then and called the manager. We both waited until he came, saw the body for himself and contacted you."

He thanked her, telling the other policewoman to escort her down to the housekeeping office so she could take a break to compose herself. "Please keep any details about what you saw to yourself." Nodding, she hurried away.

As he stood considering the possibilities, Sanchez texted him to come down and look at the closed-circuit footage. Taking the elevator twenty stories down to the main floor, he located the security office in the back corner of the bustling lobby. Inside the double doors, he found Sanchez kicked back in a desk chair, shaking her head. The somber chief of security, a tall, dark-haired man, peered over her shoulder. When she saw Elijah enter, she hummed the familiar tune of a song about bad girls.

"We got us a hot tamale," she teased as he crossed the drab, utilitarian room to join the other man standing behind her. A wall of monitors stared at him, all showing different areas in the hotel. She tapped the relevant one with one finger and pressed a few buttons. "Watch. You'll see what I mean."

He stared over her left shoulder as the scene rolled. A gorgeous, well-dressed woman strolled by the front desk of the hotel, turning to blow an airy kiss at the camera before continuing out the front door. "Zoom in on her expression," he requested. She ran it back and did as he asked. He said, "Stop," at the place he wanted.

The still shot displayed her beautifully made-up face showing a beaming smile. Sunny blonde hair had been tamed into a chignon, and her blue eyes shone with glee. He sighed. "As soon as we get a chance, better do a search and see if there have been any like crimes. She seems as if she's enjoying herself a little more than I would have anticipated."

"Yup. I agree. The slice and dice should have been our first clue, right?"

He scowled, annoyed at her divulging details about the case in front of a civilian.

Sanchez laughed, tapping him on the arm to reassure him as she stood. "Take a chill pill, partner. Ray, here"—she gestured to the man standing next to her—"used to be on the job. He ain't tellin' anyone our business, right?"

"Absolutely. I'll be glad to assist you however I can."

Elijah recognized the attentive look on the other man's face and realized she had gained another admirer. His flamboyant partner would never need social media to find a man. She chewed through them like a lawn mower cuts through grass. "I guess we better talk to any of your staff who interacted with her."

They set up a space to work in a corner of Ray's office, but two hours of interviews proved to be a waste of time. The staff all agreed the suspect was attractive and friendly, but, beyond that, they had little to contribute.

Chapter Two

Without the recorded bonus of her trademark goodbye, they would never guess it was her. That's the beauty of living in a superficial world. Everyone looks at the surface and thinks they know what's inside.

They're dead wrong.

As Cassandra strolled past the crowd walking in the opposite direction, she beamed a smile and they reflexively smiled back without considering why. She was the perfect height, the perfect weight to be smiled at as she swung her purse in time to her cheerful, tapping steps.

They have no idea why I'm in such a fabulous mood. And I'm sure they'd be quite horrified if they did.

Her ill-gotten inheritance paid for her perfect teeth, glowing skin, and the assortment of designer clothes that she wore. The sinfully expensive perfume that licked the air around her was a gift from a former lover who thought it would disguise his cheating heart.

How painfully naïve.

Unlike her, cheaters stank, the very scent of their inclinations permeating the souls of everyone around them. Cheaters and abusers deserved every ounce of pain they showered on others.

And more. So much more.

She'd simply decided to repay him in kind. After all, he'd hurt her without warning, counting on his handsome face to buy him out of trouble. She wondered, suddenly, if that was his last thought, that his handsome face had failed him. *How funny.*

Handsome faces were a dime a dozen for women like her. She should know. She'd had quite a collection through the years. Their faces were almost interchangeable at this point. It was their bodies that were different: dark and light, broad and slender, full of lovely, luscious chest hair or depressingly bald.

Men were very proud of their bodies, sometimes absolutely delusional about them, but they still expected us to be awed.

Hmmm...not so much.

They did have their uses, of course, and, oh, how she used them, much to their unending delight. They mistook it for some kind of worship, the silly bastards, and wanted so much more.

That's all there was. There wasn't any more. She had needs, and they filled them for a moment or two. End of story.

End of their story, anyway.

It was the reason she liked large cities, of course, the endless supply of men from which to choose. She chose her ninth, or maybe tenth, man by simply going eenie-meenie-minie-moe, list in hand, before tracking him down in an upscale nightclub uptown. He felt honored when she chose him, as was only right.

Whether that sense of honor had faded as the night progressed might be another story. She'd been a ravishing redhead that evening, for the first time ever, and had emerged from his bathroom in a skintight, leather teddy that made his eyes cross with lust.

She'd almost laughed, he'd looked so asinine, but

managed to restrain herself as she restrained him. He'd died too quickly, though, so it proved to be a crushing disappointment all around.

Most unfair. Considering the dedicated hours she'd spent in preparation, she'd deserved so much more. But another opportunity and another adventurous night always waited in the wings.

Early yesterday afternoon, she'd parked herself in a comfortable chair in one corner of the capacious hotel lobby. Taking a careful mental tally of the exits available, she'd also noted the spots where most staff tended to linger and chat. Habits were a gift to people like her, who learned to take advantage of things other people took for granted.

She'd already had the entire layout of the hotel memorized, as was her custom, but last-minute alterations to the plan were sometimes required. Not yesterday, though. As if destined to be her latest crowning achievement, the plan for this very bad man rolled out as the easiest one yet. Completing her check with a final wander around, she'd beamed at the drooling bellboys. They were dough in her capable hands, but she never toyed with children.

Hurrying back to her new apartment, she caught a glimpse of herself in a store window. The blonde bombshell had disappeared and now she looked depressingly average in the dull, brown wig and glasses, thanks to a quick change in a convenient public bathroom. Subterfuge sometimes meant you had to suffer that almost unbearable fate, looking not just average but downright ugly and forgettable.

Arriving at her temporary hiding place, she'd let herself in through the scuffed, creaking door with a regretful sigh.

A ravenous desire to relive the previous evening, play by play, helped her ignore her plebian surroundings. These grubby rooms were a world apart from the elegance in which she'd been raised, become accustomed to, and had now been forced to abandon. Until next time she was due a reward, that was.

Kicking off her shoes, she took a moment to pour herself a generous glass of red wine before settling into a battered chair and closing her eyes. Memories of last night proceeded to warm her body in all the right ways, like a sports car revving in the aftermath of a winning performance. A taped version of the whole experience would have been delicious, but her excellent memory would provide the sinful play by play.

Last night...

On entering the glittering ballroom, she paused to reflect on the sea of crystal chandeliers, their lights bouncing off the one mirrored wall. Dozens of white clothed tables filled half of the space. A drink would be required to get the party started, so she bisected the crowd and wandered to the nearest sprawling mahogany bar. The plunging neckline of her emerald-colored sequined dress did its job as she approached. The fashionable group of men standing before her parted like the Red Sea before Moses.

"Thank you, gentlemen," she murmured, knowing that very few of them qualified. "May I have a glass of Dea Pagena, please," she said, smiling at the smitten waiter who forced his gaze to meet hers after an indiscreet wander to curvaceous points below.

He reached into the wine cooler underneath the bar top. "Will the 1990 do, ma'am?"

"Darling, I'm much too young to be a ma'am, but feel free to call me Mistress." She gestured for him to open it and pour as the men around her chuckled at her provoking comment.

"And exactly whose mistress are you?" A deep voice intruded as the other men reluctantly stepped back to make room for the speaker.

She swiveled, in slow motion, to find her target staring at her. Tanner King was, indeed, a little too tanned, but not bad looking for a man in his late fifties. His platinum hair added a dash of flavor that went well with his dark, judgmental eyes. "Well, I'm my own mistress, of course. I doubt a mere man could keep up."

A murmur of approval from the other men sounded as she scanned him up and down, then shrugged. "After all, anyone can buy an expensive tuxedo and look presentable these days, wouldn't you agree?"

The crowd, unabashed, eased closer to hear his response, seeming to hold their collective breath in anticipation. His hawk eyes stared, the aggressive nose lifting in silent challenge. "You have a point, but a mere tuxedo is hardly what sets one man apart from another."

"Really?" She arched an eyebrow. "So, what, in your opinion, does separate the winners from the losers, Mr...."

"King." He bit the word out. "Tanner King." His jaw clenched, the only sign of anger that she hadn't appeared to recognize his name.

"Mr. King." She inclined her head in acknowledgement, peeking up from underneath lowered lashes.

His gaze devoured her, making a hungry voyage from her skyscraper heels to the swell of her breasts before landing back on her face. "And you are…"

"Cassandra Bell."

"Well, Cassandra," he said, his mouth twisting in a sardonic smile. "Why don't you dance with me, and I can expand on my point of view?"

"Why not?" She smiled at the rest of her enthralled audience. Tanner grabbed her fingers, crushing them as he forced his way through the crowd, dragging her along to keep her at his side. Reaching the crowded dance floor, he swung her into his arms as the music swelled to begin the next number.

"You're a little rough, aren't you?" She pouted, gazing up at him. "Maybe I'm looking for more of a gentleman."

He pulled her hips against his, causing a nearby onlooker to purse her lips and look away. "I doubt it. I know exactly what a woman like you needs."

"Oh, to use your own words, I doubt it." She kept in mind the news stories about the three women he'd raped, one of whom had killed herself afterwards. The legal system had failed all three, which only deepened her resolve. She ran her hand down his body in the scant space between them and gave him a glancing touch. His body jerked in response. "I'm not sure we're a good fit, after all."

Cassandra tugged out of his arms and strolled through the crowd toward the elevators. She grabbed a glass of champagne on the way there from a passing waiter. Turning her head a scant few degrees, she spied King as he shoved through the noisy crowd in her wake.

Perfect. He looked like a great white shark chasing a juicy chunk of bait.

Dianne McCartney

But how bitter that bait might ultimately taste was the question.

She pressed the up button and, as the doors opened, waved an older couple ahead of her and followed them inside.

"Wait!" King's fist blocked the closing doors. He strode inside, his expression thunderous. The car carried the four of them in awkward silence as she pretended to watch the party below through the glass wall. In her peripheral vision, she saw the other couple as they looked nervously in his direction. They scampered out at the very next floor.

He cornered her, one muscled arm stretching on each side to trap her in between them. The doors closed, and the elevator continued upwards. Staring into her eyes, he said, "I'm in the penthouse."

"Is that supposed to impress me?" Inspecting her nails, she gave a delicate yawn. "Why would I care?"

His labored breathing rasped, the aroma of expensive scotch wafting to her. "Because I can give you everything you've ever wanted."

She trailed a manicured fingernail against his suitcoat lapel. "How do you know what I want?"

"Tell me, then." He pressed his erection against her hip. "Tell me what you want."

Leaning closer, she whispered seductively into his ear. "I want you flat on your back in my room so I can do unimaginable things to your body."

She never lied. It wasn't her fault he couldn't read between the lines.

Tanner changed position, reaching with one large hand to tear the strap of her dress. He grabbed her breast as the bell for her floor rang. Her champagne

14

glass tumbled to the floor, sloshing liquid everywhere.

Cassandra nipped his lower lip and whirled around. She hurried through the doors and down the hall to her room. One hand anchored her dress in place. Behind her, she heard him as he lumbered to catch up. She fumbled to access her purse and open the door. Barely inside the room, she managed to turn just before he shoved her against the wall. Reaching under her dress, he clawed at her, demanding, "Come here, you little whore. I'll show you what a man like me expects."

Grabbing the side of his neck, she plunged the tiny needle hidden in her palm into his leathery skin. She nudged the door closed with her foot and tugged him forward out of the entry into the main room just in time. He slid, slow motion, to his knees, then toppled onto his side. The most delicious look of confusion spread over his face.

Paralyzed now, he could do nothing except stare. She rolled him onto his back and enjoyed a moment of celebration, taking a few seconds to stand braced over him, triumphant. Her now tattered dress hung half on, half off. Removing it with a sigh of regret, she tossed it in a shadowed corner. *Damn him.* That was by her favorite designer. He didn't have to shred it.

Hearing him make a gurgling sound, she said, "Don't bother to try and talk. I've had enough of your witty repartee for one night. For the moment, take time to reflect on the irony that, for you, payback really is a bitch." She smiled. "You'll just have to give me a minute to get my tools."

Chapter Three

Cassandra opened her eyes, sighing. Taking a sip of her wine, she savored it and ran a silky hand over the goosebumps on her arm. Who needed an orgasm when you had memories like that to treasure?

Wondering what fortunate homicide detective would land this intriguing case, she located the controls and switched on the television. The shocking news blared over every local channel, showing shots of the front façade of the elegant hotel with various authorities coming and going in an endless, frantic queue.

Finally, she caught a news conference just beginning. The police commissioner stood at the microphone, voicing all the usual platitudes about how they were committed to tracking the killer down. *The usual bureaucratic spiel.* His words were hardly earth-shattering, but it was the man standing to his immediate right who caught her eye.

Dressed in an understated navy suit with a rather boring tie, he towered over both the commissioner and the mayor. He stood without speaking, his dark hair ruffling slightly in the wind. His expression looked respectful but preoccupied, as if he had better things to do. The commissioner turned to him and announced his name: Detective Elijah Black.

How very dramatic. So, this long, leggy man with the soulful poet's face would be in charge of the investigation.

He looked tasty enough to nibble on, certainly, but, like all good guys, she'd get bored with him in a flash.

Still, it might satisfy any number of urges, that little nibble.

The whimsical idea became her last thought as she drifted off to sleep.

****

Long after the endless news conference had run its tortured course, Black and Sanchez slouched in the worn office chairs at their precinct. Polishing off the last of the takeout Chinese food, Sanchez moaned, "Gonna be a long night." She brightened, sitting up. "You know Ray from the hotel?"

He grunted assent.

"He asked me out for dinner."

"Really?" He looked up, wiggling his eyebrows to make her laugh. "Did you warn him that he might not survive the experience? Or maybe tell him to get extra sustenance beforehand?"

"Hey, at least I don't carve them up afterwards."

Elijah shook his head. "I don't think our killer allowed King to get that far. The crime scene appeared to be too pristine. But, according to the witnesses, the lure of sex was how she gained access to this guy so easily. The rest of the security footage certainly bore that out."

She snorted with derision. "Men are so damn easy."

"Not all of us."

"Okay, okay. You're about as pure as my virgin pina colada. But you're not a typical guy, either."

"Thanks, I think."

She stood, stretching. "Let's go take a look at her place."

He glanced at the address the morgue technician had found buried inside King's clothing. Unfortunately, they'd determined she'd likely planted a business card for the building complex there on purpose. Someone with that much panache didn't make those kinds of sloppy mistakes.

Showing her photograph to the manager via fax machine had verified their suspect rented one of the pricier units on the second highest floor. "Uptown, of course. She's going to be long gone."

"Yup. And it'll be scrubbed clean, but we gotta have a peek anyway. Maybe we'll get lucky."

"Sure." Ignoring the certainty of a wasted trip, he grabbed his jacket and they left.

The laborious drive lasted thirty minutes as they wound through gridlocked evening rush hour traffic. When they arrived at the upscale address provided, they parked their car close to the door, the police permit displayed on the dash. They advised the disconcerted building manager of the specific reason for their visit. During their initial contact, they had just sent her photo and asked if she lived there.

Overwrought, the slender, older man escorted them upstairs in an elevator, wringing his hands in despair after the doors whispered shut behind them. "This has to be a m-misunderstanding," he stuttered. "She's a lovely young lady, always very pleasant and courteous."

"That's what every murderer's mother says," Sanchez quipped.

The man shot her a look of disdain, his pinched lips

turning downwards. You could almost taste his disapproval. When they arrived at the correct floor, he led them to the ornate door. Knocking, then waiting for an answer to no avail, he opened it, handing Elijah the key.

"Thank you. The crime scene crew will be here shortly. Her apartment will be off limits until we release it."

The other man sighed, adding an eye roll to signal his displeasure.

He couldn't waste time on dramatics. "You said it's paid for until the end of the month, right? So, you wouldn't have access to it until then anyway."

"I suppose that's true." Nodding, he seemed to recognize he'd annoyed them and made himself scarce. They shut themselves inside.

The spotless interior offered the high-end designer look he had expected, given the quality building. A beautifully upholstered sofa with matching chairs in the living room and every other pristine surface exemplified minimalism at its most expensive. Sure, it would be considered the height of elegance, but, to him, it looked cold and lacked any sense of character.

During their initial inquiry over the phone, the manager had told him the now-infamous Cassandra had asked for a very thorough cleaning at the crack of dawn, paying an extra, hefty fee for the early hour. She had told him important guests would be arriving before dinner, stressing that the place had to pass her perfectionist white-glove test of cleanliness.

Apparently, their killer possessed a sense of humor.

The overworked evidence team showed up lugging their equipment soon after he and Sanchez arrived.

After a short while, they confirmed his initial impression. "It's squeaky clean," the first technician said. "We'll do the best we can, but I wouldn't hold out much hope. Every surface reeks of bleach."

He and Sanchez were just about to leave them to it when the young man called out, "Wait a minute," his voice drifting to them from the bedroom. He appeared in the doorway, one gloved hand holding a folded piece of paper.

Requesting he unfold it, Elijah stood next to him to discover what it said. Typed in a large computer font, it read, "We can best get justice by doing justice."

A jolt of recognition made him pause. "Theodore Roosevelt."

Sanchez rolled her eyes. "Seriously? How do you remember all that crap?"

"I don't spend all my off time watching reality television, like some people I could name. I read books."

"Boring, old-man books."

Laughing, he nodded his thanks to the technician. "Where did you find it?"

"On the bed, tucked under the pillow."

They waited patiently until the crew had finished their work in the hope they would find something else, but no luck. The appropriate tests would be done, but they didn't hold out much hope for helpful results.

Locking the ornate door behind them, Elijah ran yellow crime scene tape over the exterior surface. "It's almost eleven," he noted, glancing at his watch. "Let's clock out until six. We can start again, fresh, in the morning. I think we're in this for the long haul. Dr. Hayes said he'd have the results first thing in the morning to get the mayor off his back."

"Yeah, because this guy was such a prize, he deserves priority, right?"

"Getting off on three rape charges puts him pretty low on my to-do list, but he had money. We all know money talks the loudest in this town." With that truthful but depressing comment, they parted ways.

****

On waking, still drowsy, Cassandra stared at the grubby walls in disbelief until it finally registered that fun time in the preceding stylish apartment had expired. *Boo.* It cheered her a little when she remembered today's most interesting errand: digging up more information on the compelling Elijah Black.

Anxious to get started, she scrambled over to her laptop computer before entertaining any plans for breakfast. A simple online search revealed the basic facts about Detective Black: age thirty-eight and divorced. He had been a homicide detective for six years. An educated guy, he had earned an undergraduate degree in, of all things, philosophy. So, a smart cop. That might be part of the reason he'd risen quickly in his department.

Another news article popped up, one of those pieces that sang the praises of the New York Police Department, offering Black as the glowing example for their cause. She could understand why the chief had offered him as such. Those intense eyes, which almost matched the darkness of his hair, made him rather photogenic. He also had a tangible air of concentration she'd noticed on the television, as if he stayed ten mental steps ahead of everyone.

Well, was he ten steps ahead? She tossed her head,

laughing out loud. Certainly not ten steps ahead of her. Not yet, anyway.

But it might be a tremendous amount of fun to play that game of one-upmanship with him.

Chapter Four

As expected, the early morning visit to the morgue yielded nothing but a frustrated medical examiner with an astounding lack of evidence. Widely considered to be the best in his field, if Dr. Hayes couldn't find anything, there would be nothing to find.

The single hair they'd had such high hopes for belonged to a high-quality wig. Running down possible outlets and buyers would entail an exhausting and probably unsuccessful search. She had very likely paid cash. They'd only pursue that as a last resort.

He and Sanchez stood, gowned and gloved, in the chilly morgue filled with medical equipment and observed. The painstaking initial examination of hair, nails and skin had been completed. It seemed odd that the rest of his body remained almost untouched, despite the slaughtered remains of his manhood.

The doctor made a Y incision in the torso, then separated the ribs. Once he had access, he began the tedious task of examining and weighing the internal organs. "Not in bad shape for a man of fifty-eight. A little fat around the middle." He lifted the liver out and weighed it. "Probably drank a little more than he should. I can't see much else he would have worried about until you get to the heart and lungs. As you can see, it's those two that tell the tale here."

Elijah sighed. "Did he die from blood loss?"

"Yes. But if that hadn't killed him, the paralytic agent would have stopped his heart before help could arrive. I would bet she used a higher dosage than necessary. It was basically a race to the finish line between the two causes."

"And you can tell that without waiting for the bloodwork?"

"Yes. I've seen several cases like this before. The body shows a massive histamine release that compromised the lungs. Used in surgery, these things are carefully controlled. Under these circumstances, it's a miserable death. The inability to breathe starves the lungs, then overloads the heart." He frowned. "As you know, it can't be confirmed without blood tests, but I'm telling you so you know what you're dealing with."

"Where would she purchase a paralytic like that?"

"A member of the public can't get it from a legitimate source, so it would have to be a black-market purchase. Good luck tracing that."

"Thanks, Doc. Any idea what kind of weapon we're dealing with?"

He grimaced. "It's as messy a neutering as I've seen," he said, examining the congealing layers of tissue. "I would guess perhaps a pair of heavy-duty kitchen shears. Or even tailor shears. Either one would do a lot of damage, and you'd need less skill than with a knife." He paused to consider the logistics. "They're bulky and heavy. She probably just carted them away in her suitcase."

Thanking him, they abandoned the depths of the clinical dungeon and returned to the office, a little disheartened. They settled down to work with a carafe of coffee sitting in between them. Like a lot of cops, it was their lifeblood. It kept them going through the exhausting hours of an investigation. The chances of solving a murder case diminished with each passing hour. If they didn't capture Cassandra within the first three to four days, they were probably screwed. The FBI would be called in, and they'd be off the case.

A thorough search for like crimes here in the city had yielded nothing so far, but instinct and the meticulous crime scene told him it couldn't be this killer's first crime. Leaving little to no evidence was more of a challenge than most people could imagine.

He let Sanchez continue on that end of things while he took the search statewide and, almost immediately, caught a hit. Four months ago, a businessman named Stan Barber, age sixty-two, had been found murdered in his penthouse apartment upstate. His offending appendage had been stuffed down his throat in what appeared to be a posthumous gesture of retribution.

A paralytic agent had been used in that case, which boded well for Dr. Hayes's prediction. The victim's two-million-dollar home had been left pristine with nary a scent of helpful clues. The living room where he'd been found had been recently scrubbed with an abundance of full-strength cleaners.

Searching the minimal report, he saw that, according to the doorman, the tenant's only visitor that day had been a "dead sexy" redhead who had arrived on the victim's arm in the middle of the night. She'd left a few hours later, in the early hours of the morning, cheerfully blowing him a kiss. The doorman had filled in the blanks about their activities because, as he said, her kind of visitors arriving were a regular occurrence for his tenant.

Barber's last known whereabouts before the murder had been an upscale businessman's club downtown, his regular haunt. According to the report, that particular club was a well-known place for young women to connect with rich, older men. Several members recalled seeing him and the redhead together there, laughing and flirting up a storm. The case remained unsolved. He noted the lead investigator's name and placed a call to his precinct, leaving a message asking for him to get in touch. Catching sight of Sanchez talking with another officer out in the hall, he waved her in. "I found a similar crime."

"How similar?"

He smiled. "Oh, it's her."

She cut her conversation short and plunked down in the seat next to him. Looking at the scant details, she nodded. "Yep, I agree. A few differences, though."

"I think she gets bored and likes to change the details up. No mention of a note, for instance."

"You think this guy's another rapist?"

He shrugged. "It's bound to be some crime against women. I left a message for the investigator in charge to call. We'll see what he has to contribute."

A busy two hours later, they discovered the detective in charge of that case really didn't give a damn. Sam Mulvaney, who bragged about being four months from retirement, apparently filled his remaining days by going through the motions on his caseload. "Yeah, just another bullshit case," he muttered, pausing to yawn. He took a bite of something, and the crunching sound made him hard to hear. "That asshole beat the crap out of both his wives and then bought his way out of it. I still think one of them did it, but I couldn't prove it."

I doubt that he worked too hard on anything these days. "But you had security footage showing a much younger woman exiting the apartment, right?"

He grunted assent. "Yeah, but both of the old bags had more dough than they knew what to do with. Nothing to shove a hundred thousand the killer's way and all three broads are dancing the boogaloo with beach boys in Hawaii."

Elijah realized he could waste a lot of precious time talking with this moron. He'd clearly come to whatever conclusion meant the least amount of work for him.

He never understood men who made a sport of disparaging women. Sanchez, for instance, made his work life much easier, often offering a fresh perspective, especially with women offenders. "Can you send me copies of your file and the tape?"

"Sure. Have at it. You ain't gonna find nothin', hotshot, but it's no skin off my ass."

He thanked him and hung up, swearing. "Cops like that give us all a bad name."

Sanchez grinned. "Not all of us can be the mayor's poster boy."

****

Late that night, Cassandra observed Black and Sanchez from a shadowed corner of their favorite neighborhood bar. She studied their habits as a scientist would mice in a laboratory. They stopped here almost nightly to grab some dinner. *You'd think they'd get tired of this dump.*

Tonight, the disciplined Elijah ordered a Cobb salad and one German beer, while his hot tamale

27

partner had nachos, then a burger while guzzling down three dark ales. They were clearly taking what was left of the night off. Even cops could only work so many twenty-hour days.

A lot of other patrons, clearly law enforcement, passed their table and greeted them. Most of them received a reserved smile and a nod from him and a wink along with teasing from her. Their body language told her they had a solid partnership but had never been lovers. Opposites balancing each other out, she supposed.

She knew it may be tempting fate to be here but couldn't seem to prevent herself from sneaking one toe over the line. The enigmatic Elijah Black fascinated her. Not in a "you're my next mark" kind of way, more of a "I might have to jump you" kind of way.

And isn't that a kicker. She'd never chased a good guy before now, worried she'd die of terminal boredom. She must really want him if she could slum it here, hanging out in a seedy cop bar, somewhere far from her usual hunting grounds.

It was one of the great ironies of life, she supposed. The dissolute father she'd despised had left her all the cash she needed to pursue her extraordinary goals. Living the high life had wooed and won her years ago, so hanging out in a place like this seemed akin to watching hulking animals in the metro zoo.

Still, she might like to stroke the black panther across the room, she thought, watching him take in the other patrons' actions as if he remained separate from it all. Real hunger stirred, which stunned her.

When was the last time I felt true desire for anyone? Impossible to recall. Maybe never.

A short while later, the duo stood to leave, calling goodbyes and wandering to the door amidst various drunken responses. Following them out a few minutes later, she watched them bid each other goodnight and head in opposite directions. The night crowd instantly swallowed up Sanchez, but, luckily, tall people were the simplest to follow. Sliding through the occasional group of pedestrians, she easily closed the distance between her and her quarry.

When Elijah began speaking to a few people still perched on their shadowed front stoops as he passed, she knew he lived nearby. Keeping an eye on the traffic, she changed sides of the street, getting ahead of him on the parallel sidewalk so she could glance back. Stopping to pat a random dog allowed her to catch sight of him climbing the stairs of his home and fitting a key into the lock of number forty-four.

He'd entered a crisp, red-brick row house with a tidy front garden, a nicer and better maintained home than she would have expected on a detective's salary. An inheritance, maybe? One of the many assorted questions about him that piqued her interest.

Glancing at her watch, she knew the time had come to head to her dreadful interim rental apartment to finalize plans for the next call to judgement. She had conceived a rather provocative plan to complicate Elijah's life in a way he certainly wouldn't appreciate.

What glorious fun. The mere idea of it filled her with anticipation.

At 2 a.m., after finally crawling in between the sheets on her lumpy bed, she tried to sleep. Despite her best efforts, she still lay awake, her active brain whirling, an hour later. She had never slain a man in the same locale before and never one so soon after the last hit. The challenge aroused her, baiting Elijah and matching wits with him.

It was daring, dangerous and so divinely her. She might even, just for a moment, let him think he could win.

****

Black and Sanchez sat looking through the footage from the Montac for what seemed like the thousandth time. "You almost have to admire her." She sighed.

"You want me to admire a murderer?"

She snorted a laugh at his incredulous tone. "C'mon, seriously. This dude is supposed to be brilliant, right? He makes a billion dollars out of almost nothing, then gets sliced up because she pats his noodle and flashes her boobs."

"You make a valid point." Stretching, he stood, hearing his knees crinkle and crack from staying one in position too long. He often considered those sounds a symptom of tall man's disease. "Our unmotivated friend from upstate finally sent me the files from the other crime. Ready to have a look?"

She glanced down the hall. "I need something to eat."

"Didn't you just eat an hour ago?"

She swatted his arm as she walked past. "Energy keeps the motor runnin', pal. Be right back."

He cued up the footage while she hurried to the snack machines down the hall. On her return, a candy bar in each hand, they crowded around his computer to watch the DVD first. Almost identical to the Montac footage, the suspect turned towards the camera and blew a kiss at the doorman during her exit. The only difference was that she'd transformed into a redhead here, the short bob giving her a sleek, catlike look.

Afterwards, they looked at the file separately, but both came to the same frustrating conclusion. The investigation was sloppy at best. Usually, with murders, there would be one case out of the bunch that created the fuel for the others. Sometimes it might be the original target that gave them some positive reward. It then spurred them on to recreate the experience. Other times, they used the first few crimes to fine-tune their craft so they would be ready for their ultimate target at a later date.

It became impossible to tell which was the case here, because the investigation on this other crime had been carried out in such an ineffective manner. Who knew how much evidence might have been lost because of it? She blew out a breath. "The scary thing is, how many names do you think are on this chick's kill list?"

He considered her question. "Actually, I'd be more interested in knowing how many have already been checked off. She's quite proficient. That usually comes with a great deal of practice."

"Good point. But don't say that too loud or we'll have the Feds sticking their nose in where they don't belong."

The two of them worked well past dinner hour, ignoring grumbling stomachs, until their eyes blurred from staring at their respective computer screens. They'd bottomed out, energy-wise, and were just reaching for their jackets when his desk phone rang.

"Ignore it," Sanchez suggested with a groan.

Elijah shook his head, stretching out a hand to grab the receiver. "Detective Black."

"Hello, darling. I've decided we're going to be friends, so I've left you a present."

His fatigue fled as he gestured to Sanchez, shoving a notepad across the desk to get her attention, then pointing to the receiver. His partner scrambled out the door to try and get a recording arranged. Attempting to buy some time, he said, "Who is this?"

She laughed, a tinge of scorn coloring the sound. "Let's not play foolish games, Elijah. You know exactly who this is."

"Why are you calling me, Cassandra?"

"That's my name today. Who knows what it will be tomorrow?"

"It will do for now. Where are you?"

"Close by. You asked why I'm calling? Well, to perform my civic duty, of course." She chuckled. "As to where I am, well, let's just say I'm hanging out in your neighborhood. You'd both better stay at the office like the exemplary officers you are. There's no time for a late dinner tonight. You and Sanchez are about to get a frantic call to another challenging crime scene."

"Why are you doing this? At least tell me that much."

She expelled a harsh breath. Her mood changed as if flipping a switch, and he could suddenly feel the quivering rage in her tone. "Because I waited for justice, and she never showed up. Now, it's my turn."

Chapter Five

The phone slammed down. "Damn it!" Elijah knew it hadn't been long enough to discover her location. Rushing to the dirt-smudged windows, he peered out.

"What are you doing?" Sanchez moved across the room to stand beside him.

"Cassandra said she was in our neighborhood and knew we were still at the office. How would she know that if she wasn't watching?"

"A lucky guess?"

"I don't think so. I think she really is nearby."

The streets below still contained a number of people, but, from a distance, most seemed to be men or streetwalkers. He examined the windows of the buildings across the way, but the majority of them were dark with no people in sight. Frustrated, he turned toward his partner. "She said we should stick around, that we're going to get another call."

As expected, her own call hadn't been long enough to trace. They sat together, glum and pessimistic, praying the phone would remain silent. Five minutes later, it rang, dashing their hopes. They received a summons from the commissioner's office to report there immediately, an extremely uncommon occurrence. The big boss never worked late at night, not here in the office building, anyway.

Hustling over, they couldn't stop their curiosity

from running rampant. On arrival, the spacious office blazed with light, and people could be seen in every corner. They were hurried inside.

Normally a handsome and confident man, the commissioner sat on the couch, hunched over with his head in his hands. Elijah could determine nothing from the subdued hum of conversation around them and paused, wondering what had happened. It had to be tragic to cause such despair.

Their lieutenant, standing next to him, made his way across the room. Pulling them aside, he lowered his voice. "The commissioner's brother, Edgar Banks, was just found murdered at his home. The condition of the body indicates there might to be a tie to your ongoing case. We have a pair of patrolmen guarding the entrance until your arrival." He handed them a slip of paper with the address. "I'll keep him here and out of the way as long as possible."

"Yes, sir." Elijah strode to the door, letting Sanchez scramble to keep up. They remained silent on their ride down in the elevator. At last, they reached the confines of the car where they couldn't be overheard.

"This is gonna be a shit show," she muttered, scrubbing her hands over her face.

"Do you know anything about his brother? A money guy, isn't he?"

"He's supposed to be some kind of financial genius, but I've never heard anything criminal, just that he's an arrogant asshole."

At least the streets stayed relatively quiet at this time of night. They made fast time getting to the elegant high-rise. A couple of news crews already crowded the entrance, raising a ruckus that would only complicate the sensitive situation. In this day of instant access, nothing could be kept quiet for very long. Listening to police radio communications gave anyone who wanted it a front row seat.

They pushed through the surging crowd, ignoring the usual shouted demands for more information. He recognized the stalwart doorman who stood at attention, ignoring the horde, as a retired cop. "Hi, Harry. Need me to call for some help or can you handle this bunch?"

"I got 'em, thanks." The burly man wore a pristine cream uniform with gold buttons, a world apart from police blues. He handed them a silver plastic card key. "Express elevator straight to the penthouse is the third one on your right. Two of your boys are guarding the door of the suite. I told 'em to leave the rest of it alone."

"Perfect. Thanks."

The key gave them access into the elevator. The penthouse was the sole destination listed beside the designated button. On the top floor, they stepped out of the elevator into a short hallway. Everything was a soft cream color. He almost felt guilty for walking on the carpet.

The two patrolmen guarding the door looked fresh out of the police academy, standing at attention when they saw them approach. They had done as instructed, but both were pale, their eyes as big and shiny as soup spoons. Elijah stopped in front of them. "Thanks for keeping watch. How did you find out we had a disturbance here?"

"My partner and I received a call from dispatch at 10:07 saying a lady had phoned in and said someone at this address needed assistance," the taller one replied.

"The door was cracked open a few inches. We drew our weapons and went in a few feet. As soon as we saw how bad it was, we backed out. My partner called you guys, and Samson here was sent to stand guard with me."

"How far did you go in?"

"Maybe four to six feet. We brushed against the door frame and pushed the door wide open for a better look, but we didn't touch anything else. We could see enough to tell nobody else was around."

Elijah didn't have the heart to tell them they probably should have cleared the other rooms to confirm for certain the suspect had fled. Hiding in closets and under beds wasn't unheard of. All in all, though, he'd rather have an intact crime scene. They knew she was long gone, anyway. "Okay, good job. Thanks, you two. Stay here for now. Somebody will be along soon to relieve you."

He and Sanchez moved into the stylish, spacious room, snapping on gloves. The deceased man slumped, naked, in an armchair facing the entry. His legs were spread wide to frame what used to be his crotch, now nothing but a bloody, oozing mass.

"Holy crap," she whispered. "Where's his wiener?" He frowned at her irreverence but couldn't help but wonder the same thing. The relevant part was nowhere in sight.

On closer inspection, the victim had the same terrorized expression as the last victim. Elijah registered the basics—bulging eyes and balding pate, much shorter than his brother and, even at the best of times, less attractive. A man's patterned silk robe puddled on the floor nearby.

He scanned the immediate surroundings and knew he was wasting his time in here. "See what you can find. I'm going to check out the bedroom."

Pushing the door open, he paused, registering disbelief. At first glance, it reminded him of something created by an 80s porn star, not in any way matching the elegant front rooms.

The deceased's custom bed, the size of two king-sized mattresses, sat like a stage centered in the room. A quilted, blood red comforter flowed over its sides to skirt the floor, accented only by a mass of golden pillows. He looked up to see a huge expanse of mirrors, arranged in large panels, which covered the entire ceiling. An overabundance of expensive men's cologne polluted the atmosphere.

"Jeez, this guy's a freak." Sanchez's voice sounded over his shoulder. "Where are the cameras? You know there's gotta be cameras. This whole room's set up like some sicko's idea of a stage."

"Good point. Let's have a look." Peering up at the ornate light fixture, he caught sight of a small, black box that wasn't original. "One up there, built into the fixture. Very clever." He made his way to the end of the bed. The mahogany footboard had an intricate design, and it made him suspicious. It took him a few minutes to determine what was hidden inside. "Well, now that's thorough. There are cameras built into both sides of this part. And there are heavy, metal rings attached that swivel out when needed."

"Seems a little excessive, doesn't it? Like it's set up for more than just one man."

"Yes."

"Where do you figure he stashes his home movies?

You know these creeps always have a treasure trove of them hidden somewhere."

They searched the room. As far as furniture went, other than the bed, only one nightstand occupied the space. Opening the single drawer revealed a colorful set of rather daunting oversized sex toys along with two large pill bottles. Squinting to read the labels, he wasn't surprised to find a sexual enhancer for men, the other a date rape drug.

Compassion for his big boss surged through him. A family man, he was widely regarded as a person of character. This would be agony for him, especially considering that the public often judged people guilty by association. Most unfair, because you can't pick your family.

The crime scene technicians arrived, and they took a break to greet them, telling them to start on the front room first. Leaving Sanchez to wait for Dr. Hayes, he returned to the bedroom and headed for the roomy closet which took up the space on one entire wall.

Two long rows of expensive designer suits framed shelves holding all of the necessary fashion accessories. Set up like a model suite, the area appeared a little too pristine. Elijah knew there had to be more questionable items to be discovered somewhere.

He began tapping with his knuckles on every surface in the closet, starting at the front and working his way back. Everything in his radar screamed pervert about this guy, no matter who he was related to, and Sanchez was right. There had to be a stash close by. Being able to relive their sick encounters was what fed this kind of predator's disease.

Getting down on his knees for better access, he

reached under the biggest rack and finally hit paydirt. He heard the hollow sound he'd been waiting for and shouted to Sanchez, "I need your knife." Hers was longer than the one he kept strapped to his ankle.

She hurried in, handing it to him, and stood nearby as he levered the floorboard open to reveal a few dozen DVDs. They stared at them, then at each other.

"This is going to be bad, isn't it?" she said, sounding uncharacteristically subdued.

"I'm afraid so." They heard a commotion at the front door, and he stood, straightening his clothes. "Stay here. Don't let anyone see this."

"Gotcha. Dr. Hayes just finished up. He said time of death is about three hours ago."

He made it out of the bedroom and shut the door before anyone else caught a glimpse of the damning evidence. The commissioner stood braced in front of the gurney carrying his brother to prevent it from being wheeled out. The medical examiner and the other men who accompanied him tried to persuade him to leave.

"I need to see him," he insisted, emotion choking his words.

Pushing past the others, Elijah stepped forward. "With all due respect, sir, no, you don't. Let Dr. Hayes and his team do their work so we can catch his murderer. Seeing him in this condition will just upset you. It won't accomplish anything beyond that."

Nodding slowly, the man sighed and stepped back to allow the gurney to roll past. Elijah waved his lieutenant, who was still part of the entourage, to the quieter side of the room. Taking a deep breath, he lowered his voice, and said, "I would suggest the commissioner find a way to distance himself from his brother's life as much as possible in the coming days. His wife and family should also be shielded from the inevitable disclosures coming."

The other man winced, his face drawn. "How bad is it, Elijah?"

"It looks bad, sir. We found a stash of DVDs in a hidden compartment of his closet, and his bedroom is a deviant's dream. I would prepare for whatever we find to be very damaging to his reputation."

"I see... Thank you for the warning. This information needs to be shared with as few people as possible until we discuss how to handle it with the public relations department."

"Understood." He waited as his boss shepherded the group of men out.

They worked through the evidence until he called it quits and went home at two a.m. to get some much-needed rest. He barely made it to the bed, stumbling with fatigue, and slept until his phone rang at 6 a.m., waking him from an exhausted slumber. "Black," he mumbled.

"Sorry to wake you, darling. I was feeling a little lonely."

He fumbled for the bedside light and switched it on, squinting his eyes against the glare. "Cassandra."

"Why don't you call me the angel of death? It conveys such theatrical personality, don't you think?"

"Why don't you just surrender and make this easy on the rest of us?"

She tsk tsked. "Where's the fun in that? Come on. You're the first worthy opponent I've had in years."

"This isn't a game, and I'm not your opponent. I'm just a cop."

"Such a humble man. Don't be a bloody bore."

"You said 'in years.' How many years, Cassandra?" Rubbing his eyes, he propped his back against the headboard. "How many years have you been killing men?"

The silence ticked on for a minute or so. About to speak again, he paused when she finally answered. "Too many years, I guess." A click sounded in his ear, and she was gone.

Chapter Six

Once again, Elijah and Sanchez started the workday off at the morgue. A few minutes past nine, they waited patiently as Dr. Hayes recorded notes about the deceased's name and age as well as explaining the missing penis. Examination of skin and nails came next with nothing noteworthy to add. They didn't envy him as he tried to examine what was left between his legs.

"Because of the circumstances, I did a blood test for chlamydia. It came back positive for antibodies, which means our deceased either had it currently or in the past."

Elijah made a note. "Given his proclivities, you'd think he'd be vigilant about wearing a condom."

"They rarely do, which always astounds me." He frowned. "I only mention it as you might consider warning his victims about a need to be tested. We don't need rampant spread as an aftereffect."

"Thanks, Doc. Will do."

He continued, proceeding to remove and weigh the organs. "He was in reasonably good health for his age. His liver shows the likelihood of some light drug use and too much alcohol. Other than that, I have nothing helpful to offer you, I'm afraid." Putting his instrument down, he ended the recording by noting the time. "I'll be interested to see if the penis shows up, although I don't know what help it would be. Morbid curiosity about its whereabouts, I suppose."

"Does it appear she used the same weapon?"

"Yes. She was even sloppier this time, a very literal case of slice and dice."

"Perhaps a greater sense of rage for this victim in particular?"

"It seems so, although I can't hazard a guess as to why." He smiled. "That's your domain, Detectives. Today, I'm especially grateful that it's not mine."

Thanking him, they headed up to the office, wishing the autopsy had provided them with something to help move the case forward. They flopped into their chairs and got back to work.

"This is starting to look like reruns," Sanchez said as they looked at the security footage from the previous day's murder. They watched as Cassandra entered the apartment lobby, pausing to flirt with the doorman, before proceeding to the elevator. Waves of ebony hair cascaded down her bare back, exposed thanks to the skintight silver pantsuit she wore.

"Let's find out if her name was on the doorman's list and see if we can figure out how she met Banks."

"Got it." Sanchez scrawled that on her notebook. "She is consistent, other than the change in wigs." Looking up, she asked, "So, why is she contacting you? Is she warm for your form or just calling to brag?"

He grabbed the cooling mug of coffee set on one corner of his desk and took a swig, looking for an extra zap of energy which failed to materialize. "She's angry."

"Do ya think? It takes a lot of mojo to whack off somebody's body parts." She perched on the edge of her desk. "Two questions. Where do you figure she put his salami and where did she get your cell phone number?" The evidence team had searched everywhere, but the victim's most prized appendage hadn't shown up anywhere. Not yet, anyway.

"She probably got hold of a business card. We leave them everywhere." He shrugged. "It's all guesswork at this point. She'll have a plan for his pride and joy, that's for certain. Some way to add more of her personal touch. I'm sure it will materialize, probably where we least expect it." Standing up to stretch, he said, "Let's do a deep dive into the brother's life. This particular choice of target seems more intentional than the others. Like she wanted to shove her choice of deviants in our faces. The question is—why?"

"Maybe she just wants to yank your chain and show you no one is untouchable."

"I doubt it. I think I'm just a tiny part of her hidden agenda. If we could figure out what she has planned, we could get ahead of her and save the next target."

"Are you sure those slimeballs are really worth saving?"

"Not our judgement call or hers." He walked over and refilled his mug. "Why don't you head down to autopsy and see if they came up with anything new?"

"Sounds good." As she grabbed her jacket off the back of her chair, one of the clerical staff came in, holding a box.

"Detective Black. This was left at the desk downstairs. It's addressed to you." She smirked as she set it down on the desk, leaving him curious. Thanking her, he took a look as she exited the room.

It was a florist's box, long, slender and white. A note taped to the top read, "To the enticing Detective

Black, from the woman of your dreams."

A jolt of premonition shot through him as Sanchez came to stand beside him. "Shouldn't you get it checked out? It might be booby-trapped."

He shook his head. "Not her style." He slipped on a pair of gloves pulled from a box he kept on his desk. Cutting the white binder string, he eased the shiny cardboard lid off.

Nestled inside was the shriveled missing penis, surrounded by white baby's breath and assorted greenery. The components were tied together with a flamboyant scarlet bow. He sighed. "Well, she certainly does have a flair for the dramatic."

Elijah used the camera on his cellphone to snap a few pictures of both the exterior and interior. Standing, he reached for his jacket, stopping to close the box. "I guess we're both going to the morgue."

He made a side trip to their lieutenant's office to brief him while Sanchez waited outside with the box. Afterwards, they carried on to the morgue to deliver the present to Dr. Hayes, whose sole response was, "Well, that's a rather unique presentation." His dry humor lifted their spirits. They removed the mangled penis and left it with him.

They dropped the box and its wrapping off to the evidence team. Pausing at the front desk where the flowers had been left, they discovered a kid had delivered them, not her.

Their next stop was Fluffy's Florals whose colorful sticker had been on the delivery box. The flower shop was only six blocks away, so they walked, enjoying some fresh air for a change. They found the store sandwiched in between a deli and a pawn broker.

Quite small and filled with matching vases of fresh flowers along with a row of standing refrigerators, it smelled like an exotic garden at the height of bloom. A fresh-faced young woman behind the counter, named Ellen according to her name tag, asked how she could help.

Showing their official NYPD identification prompted a concerned look. "Is something wrong?"

He shook his head. "We were wondering if you could help us identify the person who sent us an arrangement this morning."

"Of course." She paused. "Oh, we sent an order to the local precinct earlier today. Is that the delivery you're talking about?"

"Yes. Do you recall who ordered it and if it was by phone or in person?"

She nodded. "I do. It was a young woman dressed all in black, wearing a baseball cap and sunglasses. She paid in cash."

"You're certain it was a woman?"

"Yes. I mean, I think so. She had a very feminine demeanor."

"What, exactly, did she ask for?" Sanchez asked.

"She said she just wanted some greenery, baby's breath, a pretty scarlet ribbon and a box. Apparently, she had a small gift and wanted our extras as an accent to make it more attractive."

More attractive? Was that possible when it came to body parts? "Did you see the gift?"

"No. The woman asked for a moment's privacy. I just ducked into the back room to provide that moment alone for her. She called out when she had it packaged and ready to go." She sucked in a breath. "It wasn't anything illegal, was it?"

"No, nothing like that. Were you the only employee inside the shop at the time?"

"Yes. David, our delivery guy, had just run down a few blocks with an order."

Elijah glanced around the shop, locating a security camera placed over the front entrance. "Is your camera functioning?"

"Well, yes, but I don't know how to work it. The owner deals with the electronic equipment."

"I know how," Sanchez replied. "Do you mind if we take a peek at this morning's footage?"

Worry pulled the corners of her lips down. "Is it okay if I get permission from my boss? I don't want to get in trouble. It'll just take a quick call."

At Elijah's nod, she grabbed her cell phone and scurried to the corner, stabbing out a number. He heard the low hum of her voice. A minute or two later she returned. "She says you should go ahead and look at whatever you want. And if you need to take it with you, that's fine. Apparently, her father was a cop."

Thank goodness for small mercies. Ellen led them behind the cloth curtain to the rear storage room where the equipment was kept. She left them alone to return to the front counter.

His partner had no problem working her magic with the recent model security system. Running it back a few hours, they saw Cassandra entering the shop. They observed as, after some discussion, Ellen fetched the requested pieces, arranging them in the box.

Left alone to add her "gift," Cassandra removed it, encased in a plastic bag, from her jacket pocket and held it firmly in her gloved hands. After placing it inside and securing everything with the outside string, she tucked the bag back in her pocket. Smiling, she took a moment to lower her glasses and wink at the camera.

Confirming permission with the clerk, they removed the cassette. Sanchez replaced it with a fresh one, then, thanking Ellen, they took the footage with them.

Sanchez continued to the apartment building to interview the neighbors about their victim while Elijah headed back to the precinct. He had to spend the rest of the day looking at the first of the collected DVDs.

He'd set up the electronics equipment in one of the smaller rooms down the hall from his office for privacy because he knew what he had to witness would be awful.

And it was even worse than anticipated. The coffee burned a hole in his stomach as he was forced to witness the deceased rape and abuse girls and women, some of whom were clearly underaged. A few were tied to the bed during the act, others had slack expressions that made it clear they'd been drugged.

Elijah left the room twice to splash water on his face, anything to stop himself from punching someone. The whole display made him want to vomit.

He received a text to meet his lieutenant at the commissioner's office. Now, it became his loathsome duty to report what he'd found on the tapes he'd seen thus far. Only his two superiors and the director of public relations were waiting in the office, dread pinching their expressions. He related the actions he'd found on the tapes in as tame words as he could manage and followed it with, "I'm sorry, sir."

His lieutenant spoke for the group. "We appreciate the tact you've shown in this difficult situation and for the advance warning about the nature of this evidence last night. Given the explosive nature of your findings, we would request that you limit the staff who have access to these recordings."

"Of course. I'll keep it to a few carefully chosen officers."

"You're dismissed. Just keep us informed on every step of this investigation, please."

"Yes, sir." Walking back to the office, he tried to imagine what it would be like, discovering you had an abusive monster for a brother. Especially in a job where you're expected to know everything without the benefit of a crystal ball.

Late that evening, he gave up for the day and headed to the bar for some food before heading home. Sanchez had already left, so he sat by himself, nursing a drink and thinking about what kind of abuse would cause a woman to go to such extreme tactics as dismembering her victims.

He knew that, statistically speaking, sixteen percent of American serial killers were women, about one in six. They were a rare breed who tended to use poison or knives and leave it at that. She clearly was enraged, but why?

Did she have a personal connection to these men? If so, why hadn't they discovered it yet?

As he finished eating, he noted a woman sitting, reading, in a corner booth by herself. The slender brunette sat with one foot tucked underneath her, oblivious to the noisy crowd. What interested him was the book on philosophers she held in her hands.

Finishing his beer, he wandered over, pausing beside her. "Are you enjoying your book?"

She looked up, startled. "Oh, yes. It's surprisingly interesting."

"And why is that a surprise?"

"Because I picked it up on a whim." She smiled, pushing her glasses up her nose with one finger.

"I'm Elijah."

"Mary." She offered her hand.

"Are you a cop, Mary?"

Her eyes widened. "No, I'm a teacher. Why do you ask?"

"Because eighty percent of the people here are police of one form or another. It's our neighborhood haunt."

"Oh, I didn't know that." She cocked her head. "It sounds like that includes you?"

"Yes. I'm a homicide detective."

Shivering, she said, "Scary stuff."

"It can be."

She pointed at the opposite seat. "Would you like to join me?"

"I'm afraid I've already stayed later than I should have. Early start tomorrow. May I take a raincheck?"

"Of course." She nodded, picking up the book again as he walked away. When he glanced back, she had resumed her previous position.

He walked home slowly, enjoying the cool, fine mist that fell on his face while he thought about the woman in the bar. Trying to remember the last time he'd had a date left him stumped. The lack of dating wasn't intentional. Sanchez always gave him grief about his solitary nature, but she had a point. Currently, he strayed perilously close to becoming a monk.

This job had a way of seeping into your pores and occupying every waking moment. That was why so many cops suffered with drinking problems and multiple divorces. He didn't intend on becoming one of them.

It was hard to deny that this job and his fascination with it had caused his marriage to end. He'd ignored the warning signs, enmeshed in a never-ending line of challenging cases that beckoned. The outcome was a shock, but it shouldn't have been. The other man who caught her eye had simply done what he should have done. He paid attention.

So, maybe next time, if there was a next time, he would ask Mary to dinner. They could at least discuss philosophy. That would give them something to talk about to bridge any awkward silence. He mulled the possibility over after he'd slid between the sheets just before sleep came.

Chapter Seven

The next morning, Elijah's mind buzzed with a dozen different directions he could take the case in. The walk over to the precinct helped him focus. When he arrived, Sanchez pretty much danced around the office, reaching up to ruffle his hair when he entered. He brushed it back into place with his hand and smiled. "Let me guess. The date with Ray went well."

She slowed down long enough to thrust one curvy hip out and wink at him. "The quiet ones can fool you. Holy tamale, that man's like a power tool. Just call me drilled and fulfilled."

"Oh, thanks for putting that image in my head." Throwing his suit jacket on the back of his chair, he wandered over to grab a mug of coffee.

"Jealous?" she taunted. "Because I get way more action than you? Not that it's much of a challenge. My eighty-year-old neighbor gets more action than you."

"Maybe." He smiled. "Give me a break. I talked to someone in the bar last night."

"That's a jolt to my beatin' heart. A woman-type someone?"

"Yes."

"Do tell. What'd she look like?"

"Brown hair, brown eyes, glasses. A teacher, apparently. I noticed her because she was reading a book on philosophy."

She snorted. "Oh, great. So, you can bore each other to death." Tossing a stick of gum in her mouth, she chewed. "Were the DVDs as bad as we expected? Or should I ask?"

His mood instantly darkened. "Worse. We have dozens of young women to track down. Won't that be fun. And I just scratched the surface on the first three or four DVDs."

"Even if we can locate those girls, you know most of them won't give us the time of day. Who wants to look like the dumbest chick on the block?"

He mulled it over. "Let's see if we can match any of them with missing persons first."

"Oh, jeez. You think he killed them afterwards?"

"I don't know. Let's hope not. The big boss will have enough problems on his plate as it is." He checked his notes. "Oh, by the way, the doorman at Banks's place called back. He said Banks told him to expect a woman named CeeCee that evening. When the guy asked for a last name, he laughed, and said, 'When you get a load of her, you won't care about a last name.' "

"We still don't know where they met."

"I know. We'll keep looking."

"The neighbors basically said Banks was plain-looking and horny. Tell us something we don't know. Anyway, apparently most of them wouldn't even speak to him."

Long hours later, they could still find no matches with missing persons. Was that good news of a sort? Hopefully, it meant the women had survived the assaults. Sometimes, being in this business meant you expected bodies to pop up everywhere, and it was a relief when they didn't.

Tomorrow, they had a series of interviews lined up with people who knew the deceased, his current secretary and ex-wife among them. It would be interesting to see if they could shed any further light on the situation.

The only thing of interest in his history that caught Elijah's eye so far was the mention of a problem while in college. The deceased and two of his frat brothers had been questioned about the sexual assault of a fellow student. The girl involved had dropped out immediately afterwards. The charges had been dropped, but that didn't mean much in the scheme of things. Rich people thought nothing of paying hush money to make unflattering problems disappear, and universities were notorious for covering things up that might affect their bottom line.

The next day started off with Banks's ex-wife.

"I'm glad the bastard's dead." The glamorous blonde in her mid-forties sitting across from them pulled no punches. She crossed her legs, swinging one of them up and down, her thousand-dollar shoe dangling off one toe. "I guess I shouldn't say that, but I am."

Hardly surprising an ex-wife would feel that way. "Ms. Towers—"

"Call me Lydia."

"Lydia, can you tell us why you divorced Edgar Banks four months ago?"

"Because he was a pig." Her sullen gaze met his. "I doubt he ever remained faithful, even on our wedding day."

"How were you made aware of his straying?"

"That's very tactfully put, Detective. Straying is

such a benign word for the trashy things he did." She worried the edge of her lip with her teeth. "A friend told me she had seen him going into a building with a very young woman. I found out he'd been keeping a pied-a-terre there for some time. Figuratively speaking, the bedroom had a revolving door."

"So, you didn't know about that apartment?"

"No."

"And how did you acquire that information about other women?"

She gave a harsh bark of a laugh, out of keeping with her elegant appearance. "I hired a private detective to follow him, the way all scorned women do."

All rich scorned women. "What exactly did your detective find?"

"That there'd been enough girls up there for him to have his own cheerleading squad. And when I say girls, that's what I mean." She grinned, but the expression warped her mouth with an absence of humor. "There was enough evidence of his behavior to get me a very generous settlement as long as I kept my mouth shut. And I did, right up until today. Even he can't sue me now."

It proved hard for him not to judge her by the selfishness of her last remark. He nodded, scrawling notes on his pad. "Can you tell me where you were on the night he was killed?"

"I guess, for once, good luck was with me. I attended a charity dinner on Long Island, in the company of at least a hundred other women. I escorted the speaker and sat by the podium in full view of everyone all night long." Reaching in her purse, she handed him a slip of paper. "Here's all of the information. I knew you'd have to check."

"Thank you. I appreciate your foresight." He tucked the paper away and then handed her a photograph. "Do you recognize this woman?"

She stared at the still of Cassandra. "No. Who is she? Another one of his conquests?"

"She's the lead suspect connected to your ex-husband's case."

Lifting a perfectly tweezed eyebrow, she asked, "Is she the one who gave him his just desserts?" She smiled. "If you find her, let me know where I can send a thank-you card."

She had nothing else to contribute. After getting the name of the investigator she'd hired, he escorted her to the door, thanking her for her time.

And reminding himself that a second marriage looked less attractive to him every second.

The next interview was with Banks's secretary, a petite brunette who scurried in, glancing around her as if considering whether she'd been followed. One hand strayed up to smooth her hair as she walked. He waved her to a seat in the interview room and sat opposite her. "Thank you for coming down."

"It's fine." She clasped her hands in her lap, unclasped them and then clasped them again. "It's a horrible situation."

He nodded. "Yes, it is. Can you tell me how long you've been working for the deceased?"

"Almost two years."

"And was he a good boss?"

She looked away, fidgeting with her hands which he noticed had nails bitten to the quick. "In what sense?"

"Did you find him easy to work for?"

One hand snuck over to fuss with her sweater cuff. "I don't want to speak ill of the dead."

He smiled, attempting to put her at ease. "It's important we get an accurate picture of the kind of man he was. That helps us figure out what exactly led to his demise and who might be involved."

"I needed the job. I have three children and my husband left me for another woman." She blurted it out as if she was at fault and swallowed.

He knew at that point she'd been another of his victims, but would she admit it? "Did he do something that made you uncomfortable?"

She blew out a pent-up breath. "He couldn't keep his hands to himself and made sexual inuendoes all of the time. I hated it."

"I don't blame you. Did you speak to him about it?"

Her voice broke. "I worried that if I made a fuss, he'd get me black-balled, especially with his brother being the police commissioner and all."

"Did his behavior go any further than that?"

"He tried to get me to come to his apartment, supposedly to work, but I refused. After that, he gave up. I guess he moved on." She met his gaze. "I was so relieved he moved on to someone else. I know that sounds terrible, but I just had to take care of myself and my family."

He soothed her for a moment, trying to allay her concerns. "That makes perfect sense. You have children to think about. If you can just tell me where you were on the night of his murder, we can let you get back to work."

She looked startled and then frightened. "You think I killed him?"

He shook his head. "We have to rule people out to clear the field for real suspects."

"I was home with my kids."

"Is there anyone who could confirm that?"

She nodded. "My neighbor came over to watch television."

"If you can give us that person's name, then you're free to leave. Thanks for your time." Two minutes later, he escorted her to the elevator and left her standing there, waiting, looking as if she'd survived a war.

Why do innocent people worry about talking to the police? They've got nothing to fret about.

Checking his notes, he found the name of the private investigator the wife used and did a search on him. Douglas Kent owned his own small prestigious firm, Kent Investigations. They had been in business over twenty years.

He called him and, to his utmost surprise, was put through immediately. "Detective Black—you're the lead investigator on the Banks case, correct?"

"Yes, Mr. Kent, I am. That's why I'm calling. I was wondering if you could verify some information about your investigation into his extra-curricular activities."

He laughed. "Your approach is a diplomatic one, Detective. Actually, his ex-wife already called and gave me permission to talk to you if you called. She's a pistol and one of my biggest fans, since my work got her a dynamite settlement."

"Did you take a lot of photos?"

"Enough for a rather distasteful album if anyone

were inclined to look."

"Any chance you would agree to share your file with me?"

"Well, you lucked out, Detective. She gave me permission for you to see all of it if you're interested. I can't release it, you understand, but I could provide copies if you see anything you need."

"Do you have time first thing tomorrow?"

"Yes. Let's say nine o'clock. If I get called away, I'll leave the file and instructions with my secretary."

Thanking him, he hung up, relieved the other man hadn't insisted on a warrant. He continued working at his desk until Sanchez appeared in the doorway. "I got a match on one of the photos."

"How?"

"I asked a bunch of the beat cops to take a look. One of them recognized a homeless kid who crashes over on Fifteenth St. They call her Lulu, real name who knows. We can send one of the other detectives to see if she's around if you want."

He shook his head. "I need some fresh air. Why don't we walk over and see if we can track her down ourselves?"

"Sure." She snatched up her jacket. "Can we grab some lunch afterwards?"

"Why not?"

Their jackets were just right for the early autumn breeze that swirled around their feet as they made their way down the steps to the street full of bustling pedestrians. A fifteen-minute walk brought them to the right area.

"Hey, the babies got a hit on the wigs," Sanchez said as she hustled to keep up with him, her boots clicking on the cement. The babies were how she referred to the new, younger detectives.

"Anything helpful?"

"Not really. Looks like the long, blonde one and the short, red bob were bought at the same place ten years ago. High-dollar, fancy-shmancy joint, but they don't keep customer information that long, so it doesn't mean much to us."

"Oh, well. We had to try. That gives us an idea of how long she's been active. I doubt that she just had them lying around."

The beat cop she'd spoken to had said Lulu's territory was close to the string of vintage shops that lined these few blocks. They strolled through the area, asking a few of the kids if they knew her. The third one said for five bucks he'd tell them where she was right now. *A small price to pay*. When he had the bill in his hands, he grinned. "Right behind you. The one with the red hair."

They turned and looked. A petite redhead stood leaning against the wall in front of a local quick stop, talking to another girl. The heavy makeup and oversize earrings helped her fit right in with her surroundings. As they approached, Elijah could tell the girls were getting ready to run. He let Sanchez approach first. "Just wanna talk, Lulu. No need to make like a track star."

Shoving her hands deep in her pockets, she said, "I don't know you." Her expression switched to sullen rebellion in an instant.

She opened her jacket to show her badge displayed on the inside pocket. "I'm Detective Sanchez. This is my partner, Detective Black."

"So? Don't mean nothin' to me." Her bravado didn't quite reach her eyes. She looked on edge, as if one wrong word would send her running headlong down the street.

"Can we talk to you in private for a few minutes?"

She stuck her chin out. "Ain't nothin' about me that Suze can't hear."

"Okay. When is the last time you saw Edgar Banks?"

Lulu just stared at her, trembling, but the other girl spat on the ground, contempt sharpening her gaze. "Tell 'em, Lulu. He can't do nothin' to you, now. That lousy prick got what was comin' to him." Tears filled the other girl's eyes, and Suze reached out to hug her. "The bastard raped her."

"Is that true, Lulu?" Sanchez said, her voice softening.

She nodded. "He asked me if I wanted a drink and I thought, why not? You could tell he had shitloads of money. But, after the first one, I started to feel real dizzy."

"Was this at his apartment?"

"Yes." She sniffed. "It's this awesome fancy place. I just knew I'd be okay. But all I can remember at first is him making me lie down on the couch."

"What do you remember after that?"

"I woke up in his bed with him on top of me. I begged him to stop." Now, she began to sob. "I knew no one would believe me. That's what he said, and I knew he was right."

She patted the girl's arm. "He can't hurt you anymore. Tell me what happened afterward."

"He'd tied my arms to the headboard before he…

Anyway, he undid them afterwards. Then he threw my clothes at me. I thought I was gonna puke, so it took a while to get dressed." She gulped. "Afterwards, he tossed me twenty bucks. He said that's all I was worth, that I was just another pathetic whore and the streets were full of them."

Her friend grabbed her hand, holding it tight. Elijah let Sanchez console her, then dug in his pocket and pulled out two cards. "This first card has all of my numbers. If you need help, just call me. And if you think of anything else that might help us, let me know. The second one has a place where you can talk to someone about what happened to you. The lady that runs it is a kind woman who knows all about what you've been through."

Sanchez handed her a tissue, and she wiped her eyes. "I never knew any cops who were nice to people like me."

"There's more of us than you know," he replied, a little depressed at her impression. He pulled the photograph from his pocket. "Have you ever seen this woman?"

She stared at it for a moment. "I think so." Her friend nodded in agreement.

Her response surprised him. "Do you remember where?"

"You know the fancy hotel where that other rich dude got killed?"

"Yes."

"Well, sometimes Suze and I sneak in for a few minutes to get warm, just for a rush. I mean, the guy in the uniform finds us pretty quick and kicks us out, but, what the hell, right? Anyway, she looked real pretty, that's why I remember."

"Where was she?"

"It was kinda weird. She just sat there at one of the tables in the lobby, watching everybody come and go. I knew she couldn't be a hooker, though. Her clothes were way too fancy."

"Do you remember what day it was?"

"The day before that other guy got killed." Lulu rubbed the soggy tissue against her nose. "Who is she?"

He smiled. "Just someone else we'd like to talk to. If you see her again, don't say anything to her. Just call me, okay?"

"Sure."

He murmured to remind Sanchez to tell her about being tested for chlamydia. Stepping away, he gave them a moment to discuss it.

Afterwards, they said goodbye to the girls, then found a tasty lunch at a bustling delicatessen on the corner. Enjoying sitting at one of the café tables outside for a few minutes, they ate pastrami on rye sandwiches. Car horns serenaded them as they tried to ignore the occasional billow of exhaust. The sun had finally climbed out from behind the shapeless, drifting clouds. "So, you think Cassandra was casing the joint?" his partner asked.

"Yes." He took a long drink of his soda. "I don't think she leaves anything to chance. She wouldn't have stayed active this long without getting caught if she did."

During the endless afternoon at the office, they were able to identify two other rape victims because they'd been picked up for minor crimes, so their pictures and prints were on file. Both hung up in his ear when he called, making it clear they weren't going to discuss their traumatic experience with either him or Sanchez. Who could blame them?

They assigned two less-experienced detectives to continue searching with the photographs culled from the first few DVDs. That meant they could concentrate on finding a connection between the known victims and searching for others.

Walking home at eight p.m., he recognized the woman from the bar the other night, Mary, strolling on the opposite side of the street. Crossing over, he called her name, relieved when she turned cautiously in his direction, then smiled. "Elijah, right?"

"Yes. What are you doing in my neck of the woods?"

She gestured around her. "You live around here?"

He nodded, pointing down the block.

"You're lucky. It's such a pretty neighborhood."

"Are you out for a walk?"

"I am. I just moved into a rental two streets over, but you have such lovely trees here. I enjoy seeing all of the birds."

"Can I join you for a few blocks?"

"I'd like that."

They dodged a few running kids, staying silent as they whooped and hollered past. The rest of the street noise had abated when rush hour passed. All you could hear besides the kids was an occasional barking dog. "I'm sorry I couldn't sit down the other night. I have a case that's taking most of my waking hours right now."

"I can imagine." She laughed. "Well, that's not exactly true. All of my police experience is based on watching television shows. I'm not sure how accurate they are."

"It's a lot more paperwork and footwork than those shows imply." He stood back to let her proceed past a tree, then caught up again. "Would you be interested in having dinner with me on Friday night?"

She turned toward him, a flush stealing up her cheeks. "I would."

Relief at her answer made him smile. "Do you like Italian?"

"It's my favorite, actually."

"Have you tried Benabo's down on Chestnut?"

She shook her head. "Not yet."

"You're in for a treat, then. Would seven o'clock suit you?"

"Absolutely."

"I'm glad I bumped into you." He handed her his business card. "This has all of my phone numbers on it in case you have to cancel."

She patted her pocket. "I'm afraid I don't have any paper to write my number on."

"Just tell me and I'll add it to my phone." Pulling out his cellphone, he entered it and they said their goodnights. He waited until she disappeared around the corner, then headed back to his place.

He hadn't asked about her students and made a mental note to do so, wondering which grade she taught and at what school. Hopefully, nothing on the case would break during those few hours so he could enjoy a respite from his workload.

****

He's quite old-fashioned, Cassandra thought, which surprised her for some reason. Men who looked that good were usually obsessed with mirrors, but she would bet he glanced at one in the morning, then got on with his day.

It made him even more interesting.

Changing into soft, cotton pajamas, she poured herself a glass of red wine. Holding it up to eye level, she realized it had the same glossy look as blood. It made her think with great fondness about what she'd done to the repulsive Edgar Banks.

She'd told the pig, as he lay dying, her true identity. Wondering whether it was that information which killed him provided an even higher level of entertainment. At what point does an abuser's warped heart simply pack it in?

She was so lucky to have caught the article in the financial section of the newspaper with that very clear picture of him hobnobbing with the mayor. Recognition had made her vomit, then prompted the devilish plan. If her followers ever knew how important being well-read had proven to her endeavors, they'd be shocked.

Cassandra toasted her latest achievement by lifting her glass, wishing she could clink it against Elijah's. Somehow, she didn't think he would understand the necessity of celebration.

Playing the part of sweet Mary, the grade school teacher, was a surprising amount of fun. And who didn't love Italian food, the perfect marriage of cheese and pasta? Other than setting up her targets, had she ever had a real date?

She couldn't recall.

Having become quite undeniably lazy these last few days, she didn't have a clue who to choose as her next target. Worse yet, she wasn't sure she cared. It's not like they were going anywhere. They leached their way into this society and populated faster than a virulent bug.

She deserved a well-earned break. Instead of moving forward with the planning of a new kill, she followed the last case in the papers and on the news, delighted with the ongoing coverage. She'd even learned to enjoy trailing the rather overly stimulated Alvia Sanchez, who drank and ate like a trucker, never seeming to gain a pound that didn't look at home on her curvy body. And, by the look of the rather smitten security chief who'd taken her home the other night, she was great in bed, too. Well, kudos to her. A woman who knew how to get what she wanted.

Just like her.

Chapter Eight

At five minutes to nine the next morning, Elijah entered the ninth-floor offices of Kent Investigations. He smiled at the receptionist who sat behind a simple black desk, trying not to look bored. "Detective Black to see Mr. Kent." Nodding, she picked up a phone and whispered his name into it.

He was expecting an assistant, but the man himself came, reaching out a hand which he shook. "I'm Douglas Kent." Although only about five-foot-nine, he had the erect posture that spoke of a military background. He wore an elegant suit Elijah would normally expect to see on a banker. "Detective, please come in." He retreated to his spacious office that offered a citywide view from expansive windows. "Have a seat," he said, waving to a visitor's chair in front of his desk.

He took his own seat and pushed a file across the desk in front of him. Opening it, Elijah began to page through. "His ex-wife alluded to a parade of women through that apartment."

"She wasn't exaggerating. It got to be a joke after a while."

"Were you surprised to hear of his murder?"

"Not particularly, but I would have expected an angry boyfriend or husband to have done it."

"Or an angry wife?" He met his gaze.

Kent shook his head. "Ms. Towers, or the former Mrs. Banks, talks a good game, but she's not the type. She took him to the cleaners instead. Who could blame her?"

"Why are you being so helpful?"

The other man smiled. "Detective, I'm very good at what I do. If I make friends with the police, it makes for a smoother co-existence."

"That makes sense. And I appreciate not being made to jump through hoops." He turned his attention back to the file and started sifting through photographs. Halfway in, he stopped, peering at a shot of the street in front of the building. Off to one side stood Cassandra, leaning against the building. She appeared to be watching the entrance.

He showed Kent the picture. "Do you know when this was taken?"

"Date's on the back."

He checked. It was ten weeks before the murder. Looking up, he asked. "Have you seen this woman before?"

Holding it up, he studied it. "No. I noticed her when we printed it, but that's all. She your suspect?"

He didn't answer, continuing to look through the photos. Sorting out fifteen photographs of various women, he asked, "Any chance I could have copies of these?"

"Certainly." He spoke into the phone for a moment and an assistant appeared. "Stella, would you please make copies of these for Detective Black right away?"

"Yes, sir." She took them and hustled out the door.

"She'll be a few minutes. Would you like some coffee?"

"Yes, thanks."

He rose to get it himself from the far alcove of the room. When he came back, he set one down for him and took his back to his seat. "If you ever decide to pursue private work, Detective, I'd be very interested in talking to you. I looked up your credentials yesterday. They are exemplary."

"Thank you, but I enjoy my work."

"Well, keep it in mind," he said. "I always need thorough and dependable investigators, and I pay a damn sight better than the NYPD."

"If I ever change my mind, I'll be sure to let you know." He sifted through his notes. "May I ask what impression you gained of Edgar Banks through your investigation?"

He sipped his coffee, looking thoughtful. "His behavior likely surpassed the usual cheater, but there was never much proof except the sheer numbers of women who passed through his door. If I'd had access to his apartment, I would guess it might be eye-opening." Watching Elijah, he smiled. "I'm impressed, Detective. Your face gives away nothing. I've been doing this for a long time, though, and I know I'm right."

The door opened and his assistant returned, handing a manilla envelope to her boss which he handed to Elijah. She hurried away again as both men stood. They shook hands. "I hope the photographs are of some assistance to you."

"I'm sure they will. Thanks again for your help." He made his way out of the office, nodding goodbye to the receptionist. Going down the elevator, he went out on the street to head back to the office.

Kent was an interesting man, likely a good connection to cultivate. Another set of observant eyes never hurt, and he had been more than willing to work with him.

Three hours later, only discipline kept Elijah from banging his head against the wall in frustration. They needed a fresh perspective on this case. He knew what he had to try, but he certainly didn't look forward to it.

Another look at that disturbing footage of those poor victims had offered one clue. In some of the earlier tapes, a second person had been recording the despicable acts. He could make out an occasional murmur of an extra male voice and someone's hands had clearly held the camera. In the later versions, the improved steadiness showed the camera had been placed on a tripod or something similar.

So, who was the accomplice who participated in the early shots and why had he stopped taking part? And did he ever take his turn in front of the camera? Was he buried somewhere on the other discs?

Only one person might know who their victim had been closest to and that was the commissioner. The idea of questioning that good man in these terrible circumstances made him ill, but he had no choice.

An hour later, he was ushered into the office and stood at attention until asked to take a seat. He noted the big boss looked exhausted with bags under his eyes, his gray hair mussed as if he'd driven restless fingers through it instead of a comb.

"How can I help you, Detective?" His voice was subdued.

Elijah cleared his throat, taking note that the ordinarily pristine desk had become littered with paperwork. "I'm sorry to trouble you at such a difficult time, Commissioner. I feel I have no choice."

"Don't worry, Detective. It's all part of the job. Go on."

"It appears from the earlier DVDs that, at one time, your brother had an accomplice working with him."

His forehead creased. "And how can you tell that? Can you see him on the footage?"

"No, sir. Not yet, at least. There is another muffled, male voice we can hear occasionally, though. And we noticed the camera moves unevenly from time to time, proving at that point it was handheld."

He rubbed his hands over his face. "I'm sure you can appreciate the difficulty involved in winnowing names down. My brother had hundreds of friends."

"It wouldn't be an acquaintance, sir. There would have been too much risk in terms of possible exposure. It would be someone with whom he had a stronger connection, although that's no guarantee you'd be acquainted with them."

"You said an earlier DVD. Do you have an idea how long ago it was recorded?"

He nodded. "We had a bit of luck there. In the background, we caught sight of a sign outside the bedroom window that was replaced almost ten years ago. So, that particular scene is at least ten years old."

The other man's jaw dropped, his color fading along with his tenuous composure. "Are you telling me this perversion has been going on for more than a decade?"

"I'm afraid so."

He smacked his knuckles against the desktop, wincing. Standing, he began to pace. "I will get you a list of every friend I can think of, from…" He paused. "From how far back?"

"As far as his university years, if possible."

"I don't know how much help it will be. After all, my brother did a tremendous job of hiding his proclivities from me. Hidden friendships wouldn't be much of a stretch." Bitterness clipped his words.

"I understand, sir, but it will at least give us a starting point to work from."

"Okay." He straightened, lifting his chin as if readying for the coming battle. "I'll deliver it to your office by end of business hours today."

Elijah recognized the dismissal and stood. "Thank you, sir." Closing the door behind him, he stopped the secretary as she headed in. "Give him a minute," he murmured.

Sanchez was out on the streets, trying to track down another victim, so he sat, puzzling about the case. Usually, people only stopped committing violent offences for two reasons. One, they went to prison or, two, they died. When the big boss provided the information, they could check it against those two things and see if they could narrow down the list of names.

He kept waiting on tenterhooks for another call from Cassandra. Was it a hopeful sign that she hadn't called or was she busy gathering information for an attack on a new target?

Working on the case, he looked things over for the tenth time. No physical evidence except for that single hair, which was a rarity. No eyewitnesses to anything important.

And, therefore, not much of a trail to follow. Just

those awful recordings. He had to hope either they or the list of names would crack this tragic case wide open. Other than that, he would have to rely on the next corpse providing a clue.

And he had no doubt there would be a next time.

Sanchez dragged through the door, looking uncharacteristically discouraged.

"Any luck?"

She turned toward him, sighing. "The worst. The girl my friend from the gang unit recognized killed herself two weeks back. Left a note saying the world is run by rich degenerates and she was done."

"Well, that's depressing as hell."

"I know. Let's hope we don't find any more like her."

The telephone ringing interrupted his response. One of the downstairs cops told him to turn on the television news. Turning on their battered set in the corner took only a moment, then he found a news bulletin. They listened in dismay as the newscaster told the world a woman had killed Edgar Banks. *Damn it.* He glanced towards Sanchez. "Who the hell leaked that information?"

"Someone at the apartment building put two and two together and figured they'd make a few bucks," she guessed. "We had to question all of the neighbors about whether they'd seen her."

"They hardly need the money."

She wrinkled her nose. "But they love the attention, right? That's all it takes. Everyone longs for their fifteen minutes of fame."

Deflated, Elijah realized he'd always known having the details leaked to the press was only a matter of time. "They'll want us to make a statement now."

"Want you to make one, you mean. Tall, dark and hunky makes for better press coverage than short, mouthy Latino chicks." She laughed. "Better powder your nose, pretty boy. You're up."

They were intuitive words. The commissioner's assistant summoned him to his office thirty minutes later. The media relations expert waited there to coach him on what to say, one of the few things he found irritating about his job. He broke into the discussion. "Now they know it's a woman, I think we should provide them with her picture and tell them about the connection to the Tanner King murder."

Vehement opposition sounded from every corner. He raised his voice to be heard above the din. Turning to face the commissioner, he directed his response to him. "Sir, with all due respect, the reporters are going to have it figured out, anyway. We need any information they can dig up that might help. Secondly, if we can re-focus them on the King murder, it might take some heat off your family, at least until after the funeral services tomorrow."

After a moment of consideration, the commissioner said, "He's right." When the media person started to interrupt, he raised his hand to silence her. "Detective Black knows how best to handle this kind of thing. He always does. In this case, let's allow him to do what he suggested." Nodding to dismiss him, he added, "Four o'clock in the media room instead of outside. It's supposed to rain."

He showed up a few minutes before the appointed hour, having freshened up as best he could in the utilitarian bathroom down the hall. On entering, the media room was jammed full of reporters, many of whom he recognized, and noisy enough to assault his ears.

Once the news conference began, he waited through the usual introductions. When it came his turn to speak, the shouted questions started at once. He simply stood there until the crowd calmed, a trick he'd learned from the man who trained him.

"The deceased, Edgar Banks, was murdered by a woman as was Tanner King a few days ago. Our evidence indicates these two cases are connected by a single suspect. We have provided photographs of this woman in your press kits. She alters her appearance with wigs, makeup and clothing. If anyone sees or recognizes her, please notify our department at the phone number provided. Any questions?" He picked a statuesque blonde standing in the front row.

"Other than having the same killer, is there any connection between these two victims?"

"There is a similarity in type, both being affluent Caucasian men. We haven't found another connection as yet." He pointed to a tall man with glasses at the back of the room.

"Is it true that the genitals of each man were violated?"

Violated was a very gentlemanly word for the end result. "I can't comment on that at this time." That question made him more confident they had a leak in the department because that detail hadn't been shared outside of the investigating officers.

The questions continued:

"Is this the case of a woman scorned?"

"Was it one of their ex-wives?"

"Will there be more murders?"

Since he didn't have a crystal ball, he couldn't answer any of those questions and he wrapped up the session. His bosses thanked him. He returned to his work, putting up with all of the good-natured ribbing on the way back to the office.

"The office girls said you looked like a movie star," Sanchez said, fluttering her eyelashes.

Shaking his head, he took a seat. "It's my least favorite part of the job, as you well know."

"While you were gone, I talked to the neighbor Banks's secretary said she was watching television with on the night of the murder. She confirmed it, so I checked that off our list."

"Good to get something useful done today."

Finishing the day at a decent hour for a change, he went home to take a shower and dress for his date with Mary. Khakis, a polo shirt and a sports coat gave him a break from the three dark suits he reserved for work. He had texted her to ask where to pick her up, and she said she would meet him at the restaurant. He hoped she showed up. It would be a little embarrassing if he was left eating by himself.

Elijah needn't have worried. At three minutes to seven, she came through the door, glancing around her as he heard the hostess inquire if she was meeting someone. He took in the pretty, knee-length red dress, accented by plain silver earrings and a bracelet, raising a hand in greeting as he stood.

"There you are." She smiled and made her way past the other diners to their table. He held her chair and slid it in after she sat, then sat across from her. "This is charming."

He liked the old-fashioned, red-and-white-checked tablecloths and the chunky candles that cast flickering light on the empty wine bottles which hung from the ceiling. The dimmed lighting made shadows in every corner, providing a touch of romance without going over the top. "The same family have owned it for forty years. If we were eating later, you might hear the owner sing opera. He's pretty good."

The waiter came and they agreed on a bottle of chianti to start. "How is your case going? I could have sworn I caught sight of you on the news earlier. Am I right about that?"

He nodded. "My partner and I were just discussing that it's my least favorite part of the job, but it comes with the territory. People like matching a face to an investigation for some reason."

"I don't blame you for not caring for it. All of those people staring and yelling." She shivered. "Don't you ever get frightened about one of those murderers coming after you?"

"Not really," he said. "We're trained to handle that kind of thing." Eager to get away from that topic, he asked, "Where do you work?"

She mentioned Saint Andrews, a school right around the corner from him.

"What grade?"

"Grade three." She smiled. "Well before they want to get into any real trouble." They paused to order, both of them choosing lasagna. Up until the time when their meals arrived, she told him some stories about her work that made them both laugh. He responded by offering some stupid criminal stories. By now, he'd collected more than his share.

They both murmured approval when their meals were served, piping hot, on large white platters. The lasagna and crusty rolls were the specialty of the house for good reason. The chef made his own pasta from scratch. Stacked twice as deep as you found anywhere else, the layers offered various meats and cheeses that oozed satisfaction. Just the aroma of it sneaking into the restaurant from the kitchen was enough to make your stomach rumble.

"This pasta tastes wonderful." Mary dug in with gusto.

"It's my favorite dinner here in the neighborhood," he replied.

The rolls were handmade by the owner's wife. Elijah ate too many of them, as always. By the time the dessert tray was offered, cheesecake and cannoli on all sides, Mary begged off. "If I indulge, I'll burst, but go ahead if you want."

He declined as well, but they lingered for a few minutes over coffee. Paying the bill, they were soon strolling through the darkened streets towards home. They wound their way through groups of young people hanging on street corners. The dim light flickering through the trees meant he kept his eyes peeled for trouble, but all remained quiet with just the hum of conversation following them up the street.

She told him at which corner he should turn and they eventually stopped in front of a plain, but well-kept house. The pale, yellow siding looking fairly new. "I'm renting," she said. "It's not much, but, as you know, the neighborhood is quite safe."

"Thank you for coming tonight."

"I enjoyed it. I may not be able to eat for a week,

though."

Leaning down, he kissed her cheek, considering that a safe middle ground gesture. "I'll watch until you're safely inside." He waited as she walked up the stairs. Turning to wave goodnight, she unlocked the door before disappearing through it.

Feeling more relaxed than he had in weeks, he enjoyed the short stroll home, calling goodnight to a few neighbors who still sat on their porches or milled around. A long sleep would be a good prepping ground for what would likely be a frustrating working weekend.

Chapter Nine

Cassandra sang to herself as she undressed, stopping abruptly when she wondered what song Mary would sing. She laughed wildly, knowing the answer at once. She sang an old tune about finding true love, investing saccharine sweetness into each breath.

During their scrumptious dinner, she had expected Elijah to figure out her ruse any second, to blurt out, "It's you," and shoot her in the heart. Okay, maybe not quite that dramatic. But, still, her pulse had thrummed from the element of risk.

A wig, colored contacts and makeup could change her appearance an amazing amount. Add eyeglasses and a higher voice and—presto—she morphed into sweet Mary, the neighborhood teacher. She'd had years of practice and now excelled at her craft.

It excited her to pretend to be someone so different from her real self. She had taken the time to do an online search for humorous teacher stories to memorize. It was essential for her to live the part of her character as much as possible. She deserved an A plus for her effort.

Did Mary ever have sex?

Surely not. The chaste peck she'd received tonight was right up her alley.

In any other world, Mary might be quite a boring type, but to her rather unexpected surprise, she enjoyed being that gentle soul who hung out with the dynamic detective. He was everything he had seemed to be, both kind and thoughtful. Where was the dark smudge on his character? There had to be something.

No one could be that nice.

****

Elijah studied the long list of names the commissioner had left in a manilla envelope on his desk last night. Twenty-two men who were, or had been, close friends at one time with their latest victim. Would it provide them with the boost this case needed? He'd barely begun background checks when a brisk rap sounded on the office door. "Yes?"

It was pushed open by one of the junior detectives. "There's a young woman downstairs who wants to talk to you about your current case."

He glanced at Sanchez, happy she was here. Women tended to be more comfortable around other women in this type of investigation. "Go ahead and send her up." Two minutes later, a slender blonde stood in the doorway. Standing, he introduced themselves. "And you are…"

"Debbie Gladstone." Her voice was barely above a whisper. Looking around, eyes wide, she tucked her coat close to her body, wrapping her arms around herself as if cold inhabited her bones.

Pulling a chair forward, he moved theirs away from their desks to face hers. "Would you like to have a seat?"

She took it and sat, tucking her long skirt around her legs, one hand clasping the other in her lap. Pushing a long lock of her hair behind her ear, she said, "I'm not sure where to begin."

"It's okay," Sanchez said. "Try to relax. You came to talk to us about Edgar Banks, right?"

She nodded.

"Can you tell us where you met?"

"I used to work for him. Two years ago, I was his assistant." She sucked in a breath, her hands trembling.

He phrased his words carefully. "And why did you leave his employ?"

Tears crept into the corners of her eyes. "Something terrible happened."

Sanchez touched her hand. "There's no rush. When you're ready, tell us what led up to you deciding to quit."

She heaved in another shaky breath and her words spurted out. "He needed some business papers brought to his apartment. That's what he said, anyway. I was getting ready to leave at the end of the day and so I decided I'd drop them off on the way home."

"It sounded like a normal request."

"Exactly." She focused on his partner. "I never sensed anything was wrong."

"That's perfectly natural," Sanchez assured her. "You trusted your boss."

"Yes."

"What happened after you arrived?"

"He asked me to come in. After that, he waved me into the living room, then he dropped the papers on the table. He asked if I wanted a drink. I don't drink, so I said no. It seemed to make him angry."

"How could you tell he was angry?"

"He kept asking, 'Why not,' and telling me I should just relax."

Elijah could see where this was going. "Did you

decide to take a drink just to please him?"

"Just a drink of water. I didn't think there'd be any harm in that. I didn't even sit down. I just took a gulp or two." She leaned forward. "But when I went to button my coat to leave, I got dizzy. I barely made it to the couch. That's all I remember." Her hands started to tremble. "Until later."

She paused and, after a moment, Sanchez prompted her. "What happened when you regained consciousness?"

Tears began to flow down her cheeks. "He kept slapping me on the cheek, saying it was time to go, that he had better things to do. I...I was naked." She gulped in a breath. "I couldn't remember taking my clothes off. I asked what he'd done, and he said that he'd given me what I asked for. But I didn't...I didn't ask for anything. I just wanted to go home."

Sanchez pulled her chair next to Debbie and held her hand. "You're very brave, you know. You came to tell us, knowing it would be difficult, but you came anyway. I'm very proud of you."

"I haven't been alone with a man ever since. It feels like I'll never be able to trust anyone again." She accepted the tissue his partner held out to her and blew her nose. "All I keep wondering is why he picked me. I didn't think I'd done anything to encourage him."

"It's nothing you did. I promise. You weren't his only target. The man who did this is gone and can never hurt you or anyone else ever again." She let go of the woman's hand and reached over to her desk, grabbing a card from a pile. "I want you to give this group a try. It's for women who are survivors of sexual abuse. Have you tried something like that before?"

She shook her head, her eyes downcast.

"I think you'll find it helpful to spend some time with people who really understand what it's like to go through this and move on with your life afterwards."

She clutched it in her fingers, then tucked it into her purse.

"Can I ask you one more question, Debbie?" Elijah asked.

"Sure."

He showed her Cassandra's picture. "Do you know or have you ever seen this woman before?"

She stared for a moment. "I only know her from the newspaper this morning. She's the one, isn't she? The woman who killed him."

"She's our suspect, yes. Are you sure you've never seen her before this morning's article?"

"Yes." She shrugged. "Do you think he hurt her, too?"

"We're not certain."

Pulling herself to her feet, she paused to button her coat.

"Where do you work now, Debbie?"

She named a clothing company just down the street. "You know why I picked them?"

"No, why?"

Turning, she forced a smile. "It's owned by a woman with a staff of women. My paycheck's almost half of what it used to be, but it's worth it to know I'm safe."

Sanchez escorted her to the door downstairs while Elijah fumed. That man had deserved the horrible death he received. To destroy someone's life by having her relive such a thing over and over was reprehensible.

And to steal her trust of men was so unfair, not just to her, but to the good men of the world who were tainted by his predatory acts.

He would have to recheck, but he thought he recognized her face from the recordings. If it ended up to be her, was there any need to tell her? She seemed to have just crawled out from under the shame of it all. It would be just another punishment for something that was in no way her fault.

So, who had hurt Cassandra? Her anger screamed of victimization. Was it one of these men or someone just like them? And how did she select her targets? They had gone over and over the lives of the three known victims and could find nothing specific except basic type to link them together.

Tanner King had been the only one who had been openly accused of rape in recent years, but his army of lawyers always managed to get the charges dismissed. The other people who accused him had never made it to court. So, she could have picked him from the newspapers, but how about the other two? It seemed as if they were running in endless circles, but he knew, sooner or later, that would stop.

It ended up stopping two minutes later when he returned to the list of Banks's friends. There, at the very bottom, was the name Stan Barber. The first victim they knew about. It gave them the connection they'd been hunting for. When Sanchez returned, a candy bar in each hand, he said, "I found the link."

"About damn time." She took a bite and chewed while he spelled it out.

"The commissioner arranged the list from most recent to least, so I'd bet this is the college friend he got in trouble with." A little online digging proved them right. "Neither Barber nor Banks had any legal problems except that one accusation when they were in university. They managed to look squeaky clean after that, on paper, at least. As far as we can tell, King was the only one who kept buying himself out of trouble."

"Maybe our killer went to school with them. Could she be the one they raped back then?"

He shook his head. "That woman was killed in a car crash ten years after graduation. She'd be too old, anyway."

"So, we're still thinkin' our killer's in her thirties?"

"Probably early thirties. That's my best guess, anyway. She has too much control to be younger, but I doubt she'd be able to attract these particular men if she was any older."

"That's pretty pathetic, but likely true."

By the end of the long workday, they hadn't learned anything else, but crossing another unidentified face off the list and connecting two of the victims made for a good day's work. He was satisfied.

For now.

****

Cassandra paced around the ratty apartment, feeling like a caged cougar, ravenous for a hunk of juicy steak. Finally, she plunked herself down in front of her files, filled with a renewed sense of priorities.

Time to get back to work.

The faces of the offenders blurred for a while, no one standing out as a priority, then she paused, sliding one folder free of the pile. A recent interest, one just culled from the newspapers a few weeks ago. Not her usual type of target at all, but maybe a change was in order. That would keep the boys and girls in blue on their toes. As a magician of sorts, she prided herself on being adept at misdirection.

The chosen one's handsome face shone from the newspaper's society column on a frequent basis, youthful looks needing no assistance from plastic surgery as yet. Born into New York royalty, or its equivalent, it seemed likely that no one had ever said no to him.

Or if they had, he hadn't listened.

His model-like looks hid a depraved heart, of that she felt certain. He'd been in court twice, accompanied by the usual tribe of lawyers that protected the very rich and waltzed away every time. People like him certainly couldn't be held accountable for the jealous throngs that tried to make trouble for him. Or, so he'd said, ad nauseum, on his endless, narcissistic social media rants. He'd personally taken on the role of king of the selfies. Ninety percent of his posts showed him in various states of hedonistic abandon. He'd once bragged about spreading sexually transmitted diseases as a joke. Hardly a joke if you were on the receiving end of his generosity.

Two young women had been permanently disfigured by their experience with him. He'd played it off as sex games gone awry both times and got a slap on the wrist, nothing more. What were a few cigarette burns and bruises between friends, after all?

It wasn't a harmless prank, but he treated the whole charade like one. His victims certainly weren't laughing.

She couldn't determine whether the judges were paid off or something else was afoot, but she knew the police who had testified were furious about the outcome. After a disturbing newspaper article on the subject stirred her attention, she'd attended his latest trial. Standing outside the packed courtroom after he'd walked off scot-free, she'd heard the boys in blue swearing in the halls, asking in frustration what it would take to stop him.

Smiling, she realized she could make them all very happy. Their hands were tied by the vagaries of law, but hers weren't. She had a greater desire to please the police these days. Was Elijah the cause? Impossible to say, but the odds favored it.

Mulling over the endless possibilities, she decided she might actually have a lot of fun with this one. A public venue involved a higher element of risk, of course, but it would be quite a coup. Younger men always believed they were unstoppable, and she felt compelled to prove a point. To paraphrase a quote she'd heard somewhere once, ignoring evil meant you became a partner in it. Proof that ignoring the young man's misdeeds would be wrong.

Didn't that make her the patron saint of retribution? The idea made her giggle. One's perspective decided the difference between saint and sinner, anyway.

Now, for the fun part. She would spend the evening shadowing her quarry and determine what kind of bait she would need in order to trap him. The idiot announced his nightly plans on social media for all the world to see, executioners included.

And she knew from experience that beautiful women were welcome through any door.

Chapter Ten

Elijah was searching through Banks's known university associates, and one of them in particular caught his eye. Tyler Phelps had been a senior and Banks a junior, but every photo from back then showed them standing side by side. They were members of the same fraternity.

Further digging revealed the obituary of the man in question. He had perished in an automobile accident eight years ago. The subsequent fire had killed him and destroyed most of the evidence. A fire didn't seem to have a connection with their current crimes, it's true, but the timing was interesting. Could he have been the cameraman on the footage?

It seemed to stretch credibility a little too far, so he shoved the name aside.

Sighing, he turned off the computer. Sanchez was absent because she had been requested to help with another homicide for the afternoon. Time to head home, get some decent food and rest. The junior detectives who'd been asked to assist with the grunt work hadn't unearthed anything new that might send them in a new direction.

On a whim, he texted Mary to see if she'd like to come over for dinner, but, apparently, she had plans and asked for a raincheck.

He hoped the long walk home would clear his

head, but, if anything, it seemed to add to the muddle. On entering his house, he shrugged out of his suit coat and hung it on the back of a chair. He reached into the refrigerator for a cold German beer. Maybe it would offer some inspiration. Popping it open, he took a mouthful and swallowed.

No such luck. Blinding inspiration kept an arm's length away.

After changing into clean sweatpants and a t-shirt, he drank the rest of the beer while hauling out the makings of a roast beef sandwich. He didn't like to cook, which is why he and Sanchez usually grabbed dinner on the way home. Still, the makings for a sandwich always did in a pinch. Pulling out his copious notes on the crimes, he began to review them as he ate. Computers were all well and good, but he frequently worked in hard copy to give his eyes a rest from the glare of a screen.

He worried about the gnawing fact that Cassandra hadn't called. Talking to him might distract her from her crimes. There was always the chance, although slim, that she'd slip up and unwittingly provide them with a clue.

Was she targeting another loathsome man while he lazed in his recliner at home? He huffed out a frustrated breath, listening to a cat's shriek from the street outside and began to read.

****

Cassandra observed from across the crowded club as Matthias Riverton sat on a faux leather bench seat, literally covered with a trio of giggling girls. One sat in his lap, one lay on the back of the bench seat and one sprawled against his shoulder. They nodded their heads to the beat as the deep bass of the band's guitarist throbbed through the scarred floorboards. Their idea of desirable music amused her.

The rich boy's face was a study in petulance. An oversized diamond stud earring glittered from one ear. The jeans he wore had been battered on purpose and likely cost more than her entire outfit. He wore a sleeveless black shirt that showed off tattooed arms. She doubted whether the ink provided any kind of profound message.

Swiping one of the groupies to the side, he demanded another drink, raising his voice and adding a pout for good measure. The girl scanned the near vicinity. Without a waitress in sight, she scurried to fetch it from the bar.

Looking the three girls over, she realized he certainly seemed to have a type. All three were bottle blondes, drenched in mascara, their dresses so short that bending over offered a bountiful view for anyone energetic enough to look. Their identical bargain-basement breasts looked like they had been purchased in a six pack. It wouldn't surprise her if he'd splurged to guarantee a matching six-piece set.

Other aimless men stopped by the table, leering at the girls, but they were mostly acknowledged by one member of the entourage, then ignored.

The shrieking music, if you were generous enough to call it that, gave Cassandra a throbbing headache. As she prepared to exit, already equipped with the information she needed, a man slid over to stand beside her, his blue eyes glazed below a mass of unruly, red hair. He gestured toward the entourage. "He's hogging more than his share of sweet meat, right?"

Lovely. She raised an eyebrow. "Jealous?"

"Maybe." He chuckled. "I think you're jealous, too. You couldn't take your eyes off the little bitches."

She gave an answering purr, meeting his gaze. "I like to watch."

His eyes bugged out. He grinned, making him look like a crazed clown escaping the circus. "Girl on girl. I could get into that."

"I'm sure you could. You and every other man in here." Bored now, she yawned in his face and made her exit. Her research work here was complete. She knew now how she could grab Matthias. It would be embarrassingly easy to accomplish.

Providing him with the polar opposite of what he was sure he wanted would be the key to distracting him. He'd looked terminally bored, poor child, but she intended to rock his world in an entirely new way.

The whole outrageous plan hinged on him going to his usual Thursday night haunt. Rougher than his typical clubs, that place had very little in the way of reliable security. She'd used the location before with great success. It had been a few years ago, and she'd perfected her technique since then. No one would remember that crime. That made it the perfect setting.

She took a stroll through the entire club on her way home, just to make sure nothing major had changed.

On waking early the next morning, full of a renewed sense of enthusiasm, she planned her shopping route. When she paused to check her social media at one of the stores, she raised a fist in triumph. He had announced his plan to head to the usual club so her game plan would work.

Cassandra stopped at a body art shop to have a

little work done. Taking her time afterwards, she selected the assorted paraphernalia needed for her adventure, only taking a break for a decadent dish of chocolate mousse as a reward for her initiative. The silky sweetness lingered on her tongue as she hurried home.

She spent the whole evening putting her appearance in place. At the stroke of ten o'clock, she smiled in the mirror over the bathroom sink, gleeful at her transformation. Blowing herself a kiss, she sauntered out the door and began to walk. The long, flowing hooded cape hid her face and outfit along the way. It was a 30-minute hike to the club, but taking a cab would be too much of a risk.

Adrenaline kept her energy high as she strode the pavement, the click of her heels offering a playful rhythm. On her arrival at the club, a quick search led around the corner from the front entrance. The niche she discovered in the alley by the back door provided a hiding place for her cape, which she balled up into a small package to scoop up as she departed.

Returning to the front, relieved there was no lineup, she paused. She could imagine the arresting picture she made in the tight leather shorts and a bustier that lovingly framed her considerable assets. The quick glance in the mirror hadn't done it justice, but the full view in a plate glass window on her walk confirmed its success. A whip would have made the perfect accessory for the stilettos she wore, but keeping her hands free was essential to her plan.

Seeing the burly bouncer break from his conversation with a customer, she walked up to the entrance, allowing the beam from the light above to accentuate her bald head. He grinned and waved her inside. She took her time entering, allowing him to take a long look.

"Great tats," he said, referring to the words she'd had applied to her bare arms. Temporary, of course, but he didn't know that because the work was of the highest quality. She winked and spun slowly around, smiling, before continuing inside.

Ignoring leers from assorted men around the main bar, she continued past, making sure the setup hadn't changed in any way in the last couple of years. A man stepped in front of her, grabbing his crotch in what he obviously considered a compelling invitation. "Come on, do me, sugar. I'm into the whole bald thing you got goin' on."

She ignored him, moving around him to slip down the hall. As before, the back door opened from the inside, providing the perfect escape route. No attached alarm meant no problems. The dark hall down the back side of the building was still quiet and poorly lit. There were no new cameras here.

When she returned to the main room, she noticed the one by the front door appeared to be dysfunctional, showing dangling wires. That was even better than she could have hoped. She realized that the two security guards were easily distracted and drinking on the job. She couldn't have produced a more perfect scenario for her needs if she built it herself.

She soon located Matthias, sandwiched with his groupies in a booth in the back. After a rather annoying thirty-minute period of observation, she saw him snort a line of cocaine and smiled. Another weakness to exploit. If she knew anything about human nature, it wouldn't be long now before he made a move and put himself within her reach.

A few minutes later, he hauled one of the girls up by her arm. She gave a half-hearted protest as he dragged her towards the limited privacy of the back hall.

Cassandra knew what he had brewing in his warped little mind and would be happy to make use of the opportunity it presented. That hall had historically been used for all kinds of nasty behavior, and tonight, she planned to expand its filthy reputation. There was an unwritten rule not to disturb anyone back there.

She slid through the crowd like an eel through water and followed the couple into the beckoning darkness. Pausing to observe from a short distance away, she saw them grabbing each other and heard the expected moans and groans. Within a few minutes, he had the girl half naked and pinned against the wall, rutting and grunting like the pig he resembled.

Moving down the hall towards them, she stopped six feet away. "Can I watch?"

The blonde gave a shriek of surprise, trying to cover her exposed breasts. *A little late for modesty, dear girl.* Matthias turned towards her, intrigue in his expression as he looked her up and down. Eyes glittering, his pants pooled around his ankles, he asked, "You wanna do her?"

"No." She moved a step closer. "I want to watch."

The girl yanked away from him, staring at her in disbelief. "You're a f-freak. What the hell's the matter with you?" Gathering her clothes against her body, she scurried towards a bathroom down the hall.

Cassandra figured she had five minutes, at most, to

accomplish her task.

"Sorry. The bitch wasn't into it." Laughing, he started to yank up his pants.

"Don't bother," she said.

"Huh?" He paused as his glazed eyes struggled to focus. "You gonna do me?"

Cassandra stepped forward. "Definitely not." Opening her bustier distracted him. She extracted the needle she'd hidden there and plunged it into the side of his neck. Watching him collapse, slumped against the wall, she said, "With all that you were given in life, you should have been a better man."

Pulling a small tool out from the leg of her shorts, she opened it. Ignoring his few latent spasms, she clamped the metal teeth along the length of his semi-flaccid penis several times, hard, then removed it. She slipped a note into his pocket. Ten seconds later, she slid through the back door into the dim light of the alley, pausing only to wrap herself in the cape.

She almost flew home on the adrenaline rush, avoiding all the main streets for back alleys. Still twenty minutes from home, she heard the screams of multiple sirens, all headed in the direction of the club. She felt a little sorry for the bathroom-bound girl who likely found him, but sorrow died a quick death. Why did the little idiot spend her precious time on this earth with a piece of garbage like that in the first place?

Picturing Elijah's confused reaction to this new scenario kept her amused as she stripped herself of her leather clothing. Tomorrow, the day would be spent cutting it in tiny pieces and disposing of it—a wasteful, but necessary prudence. She rubbed olive oil onto the temporary tattoos and they came off easily, as advertised. No need to use clear tape to finish the job.

Naked now, she stared at her reflection in the mirror. Tonight, she'd enjoyed displaying what she called her "sexy alien" look. Her bald head had been a practical choice years ago. It was how she'd come into the world, after all, and how she would likely go out of it.

Maintaining it removed the chance of leaving hair follicles behind at crime scenes. Even her eyebrows were artfully drawn on. She shaved with meticulous precision every few days. Her expensive selection of wigs had been such a constant now that she didn't even remember exactly what color her hair had been in her youth. She'd purchased the top-quality pieces years ago, leaving no convenient trail for Elijah to follow even if she left a hair behind.

She felt like a superhero. Another deserving louse had met a just end. Perhaps she should have a portrait of herself drawn wearing that billowing cape.

Suddenly, adrenaline drained away, and exhaustion struck. She climbed under her bedcovers and slept the tranquil sleep of the victorious.

Chapter Eleven

The sound of his ringing phone woke Elijah at twelve-thirty a.m. With the lack of traffic, he made it to the club in fifteen minutes flat.

If Cassandra had set out to shock him, she had succeeded. Just when he had her type of targets figured out, she changed things up. Going from her previous victim to one less than half his age was an unexpected twist he hadn't seen coming. Serial killers usually stuck to type which is how they were eventually caught. She probably knew that.

Why? Why the change? Or did her targets simply fall under a much broader umbrella labelled deviants?

Could it be boredom or was she frightened about the possibility of getting caught if she didn't change her modus operandi?

Once on the scene, he found the young man's body slumped against the wall, his pants around his ankles. Instead of the typical blood and gore, they found his rather pathetic shrunken penis with what appeared to be teeth marks along its length. The expression on his face showed mild surprise rather than terror. He'd probably been too stoned to realize what was happening until his final seconds ticked away.

As Sanchez joined him and he filled her in, they could hear a woman's shrieking sobs in the background. Probably the girlfriend, groupie or whoever had found him. They'd talk to her soon.

After having a thorough look at the body, he let Dr. Hayes declare it official. The medical examiner had burned through three assistants in the past year, and the department was stretched thin. It was time to hire another one, so the doctor could get some sleep. The exhausted lines on his face told the story.

The crime scene technicians did their thing within the taped barrier of the hallway. It would be a nightmare of blurred fingerprints and questionable evidence from a myriad of sources, so he sympathized with them. The medical examiner released the body so the morgue attendants could remove it. Time of death was no big secret tonight.

Disgruntled patrons had been barred from exiting the club by the first beat cops on the scene. Everyone stood in sullen groups in the main lounge, muttering any number of complaints. They looked like a sordid collection of the misbegotten and misunderstood. Extra patrolmen and women were called in to take their information and statements so they could go home.

"What's with the teeth marks?" Sanchez asked in an undertone. "How the hell could she do that without being seen?"

He shook his head. "I don't think they're real. Too symmetrical. Normal teeth have gaps and points."

"Damn it. So much for finally getting a chance at collecting some DNA. So, what, some kind of hand tool?"

"Probably metal, because the edges are so clean. I think you can get something similar in the shops that serve the sadism and masochism crowd."

"I'm not going to ask how you know that." She

smirked.

"I wish I was that exciting."

Elijah realized his stomach was upset because the whole place reeked of sweat, sex and cheap booze. He resisted a rather adolescent urge to pinch his nostrils closed. "What was a rich kid like him doing in a pathetic dump like this?"

"On my way over to join you, I heard something about that. According to the bartender, he showed up here every Thursday, like clockwork. Liked to score some cocaine and pretend to be a tough guy. Said he stuck out like a swollen thumb because he threw money around like confetti."

"Idiot. That's a good a way as any to get yourself killed." He scanned the room, memorizing the haphazard layout. Considering for a moment, he turned back to face her. "Wait a second. Nobody mentioned finding any money on the body." Taking a minute to doublecheck the crime scene to make sure it wasn't lying around, he returned. "Looks like someone relieved him of the cash after he was dead. Are there any cameras that actually work?"

"Nope. The other guys checked while they were waiting for us to arrive."

"That's hardly surprising, given that maintenance doesn't seem to be a priority."

"Yeah, I know. Apparently, the one by the front door has been broken for months. Management's too cheap to spring for a new one. No surprise there."

She waved toward a big guy who looked like an advertisement for steroids, standing and talking to one of the other cops. Every minute or so, he glanced at his watch. "Reynolds said the guy minding the door got a good look at her, though."

They walked over to join them. Reynolds introduced them to Jake Fisher, the bouncer, whose massive arm muscles tested the boundaries of his t-shirt sleeves. His dark, burnished skin accented his heavy-lidded eyes.

"You got a good look at the woman in question?" Elijah asked.

He nodded. "She was a pretty hot lookin' bitch. Slammin' body. Turned a lot of heads, mine included."

"Can you give us more details?"

He huffed a sigh, shifting his booted feet in restless protest. "I already told your pal."

"Now, you can tell me." He took out his pad and pen.

"She was bald, close to six feet in spike heels, leather chest plate and shorts, tats."

Elijah paused, trying to visualize. "Are you sure it was a woman?"

His grin exposed a gold tooth. "Give me some cred, man. I see all kinds here. I know the difference between a bitch and a dude."

"Curvy or skinny?" Sanchez asked.

"Serious curves and her boobs were homegrown, not fake. Don't see mucha that around here."

"I don't suppose you saw the tattoos clearly."

He yawned, scratching his shaved head. "Yeah. Well, sort of. Something about justice on one arm. The other one said 'Eli' or something like that. Just writing, no real artwork, down both arms." He yawned again. "Can I go home? I'm beat."

"Yes." He handed him a business card. "Give your contact information to Officer Reynolds and call me if you think of anything else that might help."

Sanchez raised an eyebrow as the other men walked away. "So, now she's wearing your name on her body? Do you think the tats are real?"

"I doubt it. I think it's just another way to taunt us." He shrugged. "She was probably aware that the bouncer had tats himself. People with bodywork tend to notice each other, so she knew it would get back to me."

"We could canvass tattoo parlors."

"I think it's a waste of our time. She'd have paid cash. I think she wants us to chase it, knowing it's a dead end."

"I wouldn't have said a guy this young was her type of victim. Why the sudden change?"

"I don't know. Just to throw us off track, I think, or maybe give herself an extra dose of adrenaline. She's basically a junkie at this point. The increasing risk turns her on."

"This is the first time she's carried out a murder in the open like this as far as we know. Is she getting over-confident?"

He pulled her to a quieter corner for privacy, lowering his voice. "It might be just the opposite. I'm wondering if she wants to get caught. She's taking a lot more unnecessary risks."

"Then why keep doin' it? Why not turn herself in?"

"I'm not sure, but she vacillates between trumpeting her victories and sounding angry or depressed. She might be tired. If this has gone on for as long as we think it has, it might just be simple fatigue."

She gaped at him. "You sound like you feel sorry for her. You turnin' into a bleeding heart all of a sudden?"

"No, but it makes me wonder what her past was like. We both know that most of these offenders had horrendous childhoods."

"No excuse to slaughter people even if they're assholes. If we slaughtered all the assholes, we'd never have time for anything else."

"I know." They moved across the cavernous room to speak to the shaken girl who'd found him. Old, caked mascara was crumbling down her cheeks. The sum of her opinion that the suspect was a "freak" didn't help them much. Neither did her wacky speculation about why someone would do such a thing. They reached the conclusion that she didn't have anything of substance to add.

They moved to other witnesses and worked through each of the groups of customers, releasing them one at a time. Many had seen Cassandra, but beyond similar descriptions, had nothing to add. Those that weren't stoned were hungover at the very least and not interested in pushing their limited intellect in order to help.

As far as they could discern, only one witness had spoken to her. He looked like the picture you'd find if you looked up "scumbag" in the dictionary. His greasy hair and body odor had them taking a step back. Even so, halitosis wafted over as he opened his mouth.

"She wasn't into men. Showed her my junk and she walked right by," he added, acting like his offering should have been taken into consideration. "She was starin' at that trio of blonde chicks." They took note of his information, knowing they would probably never need it.

"Do you think she's a lesbian?" Sanchez let doubt creep into her words.

"I think it's more likely they were the best tools for her to utilize. Did you notice his three companions were pretty much a matched set? It probably amused her. It might be why she chose to distract him with such an outrageous look."

Leaving the remainder of the interviews to the other detectives, they headed straight for some breakfast at a local dive. A few more stops, one of them to fill the lieutenant in, then they headed to the morgue. Dr. Hayes, looking overtired and rather cranky, was just getting ready to start. He agreed the marks on the victim's appendage had been applied with a tool of some sort. He also agreed with Elijah that it was probably metal because of the clean lines.

Opening the body up, they found more wear on the organs than was normal for such a young man. "Drugs and alcohol," he murmured, shaking his head. "The young always believe they'll live forever." When they were done with the autopsy, he stepped away from the table. "We found a note stuffed deep in his pocket." Reaching into a plastic bag, he opened it to show him. He held it up. It read "The more money, the less virtue."

"Thoreau," Elijah said.

"Correct. Another one to add to your file." He sighed. "Beyond that, I can't give you anything more to go on until after the autopsy, as you two are well aware." They recognized a dismissal when they heard it. Obviously, they weren't the only ones frustrated by these crimes.

Driving back to the office through light traffic, they

discussed the details of the case until his cellphone rang. Premonition had him yanking the car into a rare vacant spot by the curb.

"Detective Black."

"Poor baby. You sound tired."

He heard the smirk in Cassandra's tone, and it irritated him. "That's what happens when I don't get a good night's sleep." Putting the phone on speaker mode, he asked, "Why the change, Cassandra? He was just another misguided kid."

"A pampered little prick, you mean. He walked away from crimes twice with nothing more than a slap on the hand. I did you a favor."

"Is that how you justify this violence? By saying you're doing the world a favor?"

"Not the world, Elijah. You." She paused. "How about you, Sanchez? As a woman, do you view the situation differently?"

The question caught his partner by surprise, but she answered. "Nah, me and Elijah are simpatico on following the rules. You gotta believe in the system. It's the only thing we have."

"True blue until the end. What a pair. You're going to put me to sleep." A bitter edge colored her words.

Elijah broke in. "Who was your first, Cassandra? And why did he have to die?'

They waited for almost a minute before she replied.

"My daddy was a very bad man," she whispered. "Like all of the others, he deserved what he got." The phone clicked off.

Chapter Twelve

They finally battled their way back into the rushing stream of traffic. Hurrying back to the office took fifteen minutes. As soon as they arrived, Elijah sat and scribbled down Cassandra's words, always grateful for his excellent memory.

"Do ya think her first kill really was her old man?" Sanchez stood with her hands on her hips, looking doubtful.

Elijah nodded. "It had the ring of truth. And do you see now what I meant about her sounding tired?"

"Yup. She started out the way I expected, and then she sounded…lost and angry, I guess. Like a kid."

"Exactly. It might be simple fatigue, or it could be declining mental status. It's too early to tell."

They took time to check the taxicab and rideshare companies to see if someone fitting their suspect's description had paid a driver for either drop off or pickup at the club. No dice. He knew she wouldn't make it that easy for them, but they couldn't afford to miss any of the necessary steps. Had she used her own car if she had one or walked? He made a note to check security cameras on the surrounding neighborhood businesses. He would bet she walked.

As they were discussing how to proceed, they were called into their lieutenant's office for a briefing. "You're certain it's the same woman?" he asked. "This young man seems like a complete contrast to her other victims."

"Yes, sir." He told him about the latest phone call and their conclusions.

"And she's not just taking credit for the crime?"

"No, sir. In our opinion, it's definitely one of hers."

He nodded, looking resigned. "The boy's parents are on the way here. They're friends of the mayor, and he requested that we speak with them personally. Can you stay and inform them of the basic details? They are...understandably distraught."

Although it sounded like an invitation, Elijah knew better.

When the parents arrived, he understood immediately why their young victim had turned out so badly. The father, dressed in a five-thousand-dollar designer suit, stormed in the door, letting it crash against the wall, leaving his wife to trail behind. "I demand to know who is responsible for this travesty!"

His lieutenant, always soothing in the face of drama, tried to persuade him to take a seat. "I'll sit when I'm damn well ready to sit." Pacing back and forth in between them, he asked, "And who the hell are these two morons?" He stabbed an arm in their direction.

Introductions were made, but it failed to calm him. "So, these are the two losers who failed to stop this murderous bitch before now?"

Apparently, even friends of the mayor had to be taught basic manners. "Mr. Riverton. I understand this is a difficult time for both you and your wife, but you need to take a seat and calm down." His boss locked eyes with the other man and motioned to the nearby seats.

He yanked a chair over and sat, eyes glaring. His subdued wife sat next to him, slumping and teary, making no effort to touch or console him.

Not much love there, Elijah thought, struggling to keep any sign of cynicism off his face.

His lieutenant offered the parents an edited version of their initial findings. "Have you ever seen the woman I described around your son before?"

"Of course not," he huffed. "She's the very opposite of anyone my son would be seen with in public. Like us, he had very high standards." His fingers clenched. "I demand to see my son's body. This meeting is a total waste of my time."

"You can see him as soon as the medical examiner is finished with the autopsy. Every minute counts in this type of investigation."

"I refuse to allow such a barbaric thing!"

"Unfortunately, you aren't given any choice in the matter. It's required in all murder cases in order to discover clues about the assailant." He wisely kept silent about the fact that it would likely be a futile task due to the lack of physical evidence from the other autopsies.

At that point, he and Sanchez were excused. They ignored the slurs the father hurled at their backs as they exited the room. "Like father, like son, apparently," Sanchez murmured as they entered the elevator. "I feel sorry for the poor wife."

"Don't waste your pity. I'm quite confident she didn't marry him for his winning personality."

Surprise crossed her face. "Jeez, bud. That's the most cynical thing I've ever heard you say."

"Am I wrong?"

"Nah, I'm pretty sure you hit it dead on the money." He and Sanchez went together to check the surrounding businesses for security cameras. It amazed them how many had cameras that weren't connected to anything on the hope that just the sight of the camera would scare criminals off. That common ploy rarely worked.

They finally located a clothing store across the street from the club that had a good, functioning security system. A helpful clerk called the manager over who readily agreed to let them look at the tape from the previous night. He and Sanchez sat crammed together in a storage room, viewing the footage. After twenty minutes, he said, "Stop."

She backed it up and ran it again. Forty minutes before the murder, a tall figure hurried by, clad head to toe in a black cloak. All you could see besides the cape were spike heels and ankles. "That's her," he said. "Why is she walking past the entrance?"

"Maybe she's just checking to see if there's a lineup." They ran it slowly from that point, seeing her return a few moments later without the cloak.

"She dumped the cloak somewhere, so she could make a memorable entrance." He noticed the bouncer take a close look at her. With an enthusiastic grin, he waved her inside. "She made sure he saw the tats. I bet she picks up the cape again on her way out. She needed to stand out at the club, but disappear on the streets."

Sure enough, after the murder, she appeared from around the corner, cocooned once again in the cloak. She strode down the sidewalk, ducking into the first alley before disappearing out of view. "She couldn't take the chance of a cab ride, so she used the alleys to avoid most of the cameras. Even if we caught her, we'd have a devil of a time proving that was her." They collected the tape, anyway, knowing all it would do was help their timeline.

Back at their office, they sat and took a few minutes to return calls which had come in during their absence. After they were caught up, Elijah said, "I think our time would be best spent doing a deep dive into that list of names the commissioner gave us. The other detectives can do the legwork on this latest case. Whether the parents like it or not, it doesn't appear as if their son's case is going to add much information to what we already have."

Sanchez reached into her desk and pulled out a chocolate bar, stripping off the shiny, silver wrapping. It made a crinkling sound as she balled it up and shot it into the wastepaper basket. "I'll take the first half of the list. Fair deal?"

"Yes." He researched for hours, stopping for a break only when Sanchez tossed a sandwich onto his desk and set a cola next to it.

"Eat."

"Thanks." He ate enough to keep going, ignoring the fact that it tasted like cardboard.

After mulling over the list, he came upon the name of a person who might fit their parameters. David Sutcliffe, an accountant in one of the big downtown firms, had been attacked in a scuzzy alley downtown and died from his injuries. The assailant had never been found. Sutcliffe had two daughters, aged twenty-eight and thirty, both of whom still resided in the city. His wife managed a fashion boutique downtown.

111

"Let's see what we can pull up about his murder." Sanchez stood alongside to lean over his shoulder. The newspaper coverage gave them little else. The man had been beaten to death, probably with a baseball bat. The police report confirmed the details of the crime, but added nothing new, meaning the crime remained unsolved.

"Doesn't sound like our girl," Sanchez said. "Not many of us ladies have the physical power to overcome a man that way."

"The wife and one of the daughters don't work too far from here. I think it's worth a visit. Even if it's not connected, we can at least slice one name off the list."

The cutting wind was rising, bringing a cold snap which reminded them that winter loomed in the not-too-distant future. Weighing the chill against the promise of warmth, they decided to drive.

Easy to locate, the elegant boutique had haute couture dresses which likely cost more than their combined monthly salaries in the colorful front window. When they asked for the manager, the fashionable clerk looked down her nose and said, "May I tell her who is waiting?"

Their badges provoked an immediate change in attitude. She hustled them down a long narrow hall, intent in getting them out of the customers' sight. They entered a rear office where a petite, elegant woman sat at a huge, ivory colored desk. Framed fashion prints on the wall behind her provided a stylish backdrop. He and Sanchez were introduced, and Mrs. Sutcliffe waved her assistant away.

"Please have a seat." She gestured to the two floral upholstered chairs opposite her desk. As they settled, she leaned forward and asked, "What can I do for New York's finest this morning?"

Glad to find a pleasant welcome for a change and hoping it would last, Elijah smiled. "Detective Sanchez and I are investigating a case and hoped you might be able to help."

"Well," she answered, clasping her hands in her lap. "That certainly piques my curiosity. I'm not sure how I can help, but I'm certainly willing to try."

"Thank you. It came up in our reports that your late husband was acquainted with Edgar Banks, a victim in a recent homicide. Is that correct?"

She nodded. "They had occasional business dealings through the last few years."

"Did they ever socialize?"

A look of distaste passed over her face, quickly smothered. "I believe they had drinks from time to time."

"Did you ever accompany them?"

She cleared her throat. "I hate to speak ill of the dead, Detective, but I found Mr. Banks quite crass. I had no interest in spending time in his company."

"Can you expand on that comment, ma'am? Why, exactly, did you dislike him?"

She pursed her lips. "The man did not respect the bounds of propriety. He made a full-time sport of leering at women young enough to be his daughter, or even teenagers. It made me most uncomfortable. Eventually, even my husband tired of his company."

"Why do you say eventually? Did something specific happen?"

"To be honest with you, I'm not entirely certain. Shortly before his death, David came home, rather upset, and referred to that man as a disgusting pig. When I inquired about what had happened, he said he'd been invited to a party which had—how did he put it—been eye-opening in the worst possible way." She met Elijah's gaze. "He refused to say anything else, but he didn't sleep well for weeks afterwards. When we ran into Banks again, he walked right by him and wouldn't even acknowledge him, let alone speak to him."

"I see. May I ask how you would describe your late husband?"

She sighed. "He was, essentially, a good man, despite his gambling."

Nothing in the newspaper articles about that. "How extensive was his gambling problem?"

"Bad enough that we lost our home and most of our savings shortly before his death. Bad enough that it could quite possibly have been responsible for getting him killed. That's speculation on my part, of course, but the police considered it a possibility."

"I apologize for dredging up all these unpleasant memories again."

She smiled. "Don't worry about it. We survived. I've managed to turn things around for myself, and my daughters are on their own now."

Thanking her for her time, they prepared to leave, only to be interrupted by the two daughters. Carbon copies of their stylish mother, they came to the door, inquiring about lunch. After brief introductions, he and Sanchez left.

Back out on the street, he headed to the car as his partner trailed behind. "They're both way too short to be our girl." She sounded disappointed.

"That's true. The story doesn't fit, anyway. We can

at least drop a name from the list." They reached the car and climbed in.

"What do you think happened between him and Banks?" Sanchez started the car and waited for a break in traffic before heading back to the precinct.

"I think our accountant found himself intrigued by the idea of illicit sex, but shocked by the reality. I'd bet Banks invited him to participate and what he found there freaked him out."

"That was my take, too."

Back at the office, they worked down the list, ticking names off after finding out the men were either gay, had no children or were still living. Towards the end of the day, almost finished and running out of hope, he came across a person with potential he'd looked at before. "You know this guy, Tyler Phelps?"

"Is he the one who died in the car crash?"

"Yes." Taking a sip of his drink, he continued. "Initially, I thought that including him as a possibility might be a stretch, but here's something interesting to consider. Even though the crash appeared to be a normal accident on the surface, the investigator noted an unusual amount of damage to the victim's lower body."

"That's weird. What kind of damage?"

"Much more severe burns than the rest of his body. The experts voiced speculation that the fire started there. The victim smoked, but that one fact shouldn't have accounted for the severity of it, even if he dropped a cigarette in his lap."

"No mention of an accelerant?"

"They checked, but according to the report, they couldn't smell anything either at the scene or afterwards. And further testing had been considered inconclusive because the fire did so much damage. The medical examiner eventually deemed it an accidental death. I'm wondering if that might have been a rush to judgement."

"How old was Phelps when the crash happened?"

"Forty-two."

"Hmm… His age fits our profile. Anybody else in the car when it crashed?"

"No."

"Married?"

He shook his head. "But here's something else we should consider. What if he had a child out of wedlock?"

Shoving the rest of the chocolate bar in her mouth made him wait for a response as she chewed. "Didn't think about that. And, when it comes down to it, there has to be accelerants that don't smell, right?" She wiped her mouth with a napkin. "It's worth checking out. We're running out of possibilities."

It meant another visit to the commissioner, but he had no choice. Waiting until the big boss was almost ready to leave for the day, he suggested Sanchez should see if she could rule out the last few names on the list.

He found the commissioner in his office, packing up his briefcase. "Tyler Phelps? I didn't know him well, but I remember him. A good-looking man, polished and well-spoken." He paused. "My wife didn't like him much, though. Can't remember why."

"It might be important. Would you mind asking her, sir? I would appreciate her perspective. Any small detail might help."

"You don't think he could have been wrapped up

in this mess, do you? He hardly seems the type." Suddenly, he turned, a spasm of pain marring his expression. "What am I saying? I was certainly wrong about my brother. Are you certain Phelps is involved?"

"Impossible to know at this point. He fits a few of our parameters. We are following every avenue of investigation, however small."

"I can't imagine it, but I'm prepared to help any way I can. I'll ask her tonight."

"I appreciate that, sir." Bidding him goodnight, he returned to the office. After another couple of hours, he and Sanchez gave up and headed to the tavern for a late dinner.

He didn't expect to see Mary curled up in the same booth of the bar she'd been in before with yet another book. She looked up at his greeting. "Oh, hi, Elijah." Her gaze shifted to Sanchez, and he made introductions. "What's your first name?"

His partner squirmed. "Sanchez is good. It's a cop thing."

"Oh, okay." Mary laughed. "Why don't you two join me?"

"I'm waitin' on Ray, but I can sit and yak for a few minutes."

"Is Ray your boyfriend?"

She flushed. "Well, yeah, we're knockin' boots."

They settled onto the opposite bench. After he and Mary ordered some dinner, she asked his partner, "So, you have to tell me. What is he like to work with?"

"So-so." She lifted a hand, smirking, to brush him off. "Nah, he's not bad for a guy."

"How long have you two worked together?"

"Since he joined homicide. 'Bout six years now,

117

right?" Turning to him, she said, "He adds a little class to my jet engine. And he deals with the brass so I don't have to." She grabbed her beer as the waitress delivered it and took a big swig. "Heard you're a teacher."

"I'm afraid it's a little boring compared to what you both do."

"Nope. I pretty much owe my life to my teachers," Sanchez replied. "They kept my ass in line when my parents didn't give a damn."

"Oh, I'm sorry."

She shrugged. "Don't be sorry. I turned out okay." Brightening suddenly, she stared across the crowded room towards the door. "There's Ray." She slapped Elijah's arm and nodded at Mary, grabbing her beer. "Gotta go. Nice to meetcha."

He watched his partner reach Ray and lay a big kiss on one cheek, hustling him into a darkened booth at the back.

"Well, she seems fun."

He chuckled. "She's a real character, but a damn good cop. I'm better with strategy and she's great with victims. We have different strengths, so it works."

"Were you ever more than partners? Or is that a tactless question?"

He shook his head. "Not tactless and the answer is no. We'd kill each other in a heartbeat. She doesn't have a clue how to slow down and that's how I like to live."

"Slow?"

"Yes."

"Is that a reaction to the frantic pace of your job?"

After thinking about it for a minute, he said, "Yes. It can be stressful work, so you're right. I guess it's how I adapted in order to maintain my sanity."

"How about your family? Do they live close by?"

"Don't have any, I'm afraid. I'm an only child. My parents were killed eight years ago in a car accident. I inherited the house and stayed because I always liked the neighborhood. It's close enough that I can walk to work if I feel like it."

"I'm so sorry for your loss." Their sandwiches were delivered, and they paused to eat.

"How about your family?"

Her nails tapped against the table. "Same as you, actually. Only child. My parents died separately, but they've been gone a long while."

"Do the kids fill a void for you?"

She looked at him with a blank expression as if he spoke a foreign language.

"The kids at school, I mean. Your students."

She turned away. He worried he'd upset her, but then she turned back, nodding. "Yes, I guess the children do help fill the empty spaces. I've never thought of it in those terms."

Their conversation fizzled after her response. They ate the last bite of dinner and left, waving at Sanchez and Ray on the way out. Mary remained silent all the way home. When they stopped in front of her place, he apologized for upsetting her.

"You didn't upset me." Moving closer, she kissed his cheek. "I'm just tired. The kids were a real handful today."

"Would you like to do something on the weekend?"

"Sure." She smiled. "Call me Friday, and let me know when and where."

"I'll do that." After she disappeared inside, he walked home, stopping to pat one of the neighbor's dogs. He enjoyed Mary's company, but she kept her emotions to herself. He couldn't read her the way he could some people. Having been accused of the same thing, he couldn't complain.

Maybe that was why he liked her. He had never forced himself to rush creating a relationship with any woman, preferring it to evolve more naturally over time rather than rushing it. In the past, when he'd forced himself to follow a speedier timetable, it had ended in disaster. He exemplified the tortoise, not the hare. The lightning speed at which people chose to live often created an excess of drama. He had enough of that at work.

The issue made him consider Sanchez and her new boyfriend. Whether Ray knew it or not, he probably wouldn't last a month. His partner approached her relationships in terms of quantity, not quality. He used to joke about him slipping something into her lunch to quell her appetites, but, what the hell, it seemed to work for her.

No wonder she thought he was boring.

Chapter Thirteen

Elijah had just settled down behind his desk the next morning when the commissioner summoned him to his office. The secretary hustled him inside to find his boss alone.

"Thanks for coming so quickly. I'd like to get this over with before my workday gets more hectic." He cleared his throat, his habit before bringing up a difficult subject. "Apparently, my wife heard recurring gossip about Tyler Phelps that I was not aware of at the time. He supposedly made a young woman pregnant while they were both university students."

"I see." Premonition rippled through his body. "Does she know the woman's name?"

"Just a first name. Elyse. My wife only remembered because she had a friend with that name. Phelps met the woman in one of his classes, though, so that should help narrow the search."

"It should make it easy to find her. Thank you, sir."

"There's more, I'm afraid, and it's quite horrendous. It's also unproven and may be vicious gossip for all I know. I don't usually repeat such inflammatory information, but it may prove to be pertinent to our case."

"Understood."

"Initially, Phelps would have nothing to do with his illegitimate child, even refusing to pay basic support.

However, he took his young daughter into his home when she was twelve, because her mother died of cancer."

His boss stood and paced to the window to look out, the restless action demonstrating his discomfort. "The daughter was reputed to be quite beautiful." He turned to face him, his eyes haunted. "Over time, a few observers voiced their concern that Phelps might be involved in an unnatural relationship with his daughter. A former maid supposedly quit before reporting him for suspicious actions involving the child. The authorities brushed it off as the revenge plan of an ex-employee, an explanation offered by Phelps."

"I see."

"It's most upsetting. Lately, nothing is as it seems. Just mentioning the whole affair upset my wife, even after all these years."

He could only imagine how awkward that conversation must have been. "I can understand how you both feel, sir, but this is very helpful information we couldn't have heard from anyone else."

"Do you think there's a chance that poor child became our murderer?"

"I'm not sure, but it's a great lead to follow, the first truly worthwhile one we've had. Does your wife know the daughter's name?"

"No, but apparently she inherited her father's entire, rather substantial, estate, so she should be listed as beneficiary in those legal files." A glimmer of a smile crossed his face. "I can see you're eager to run this down, so you're dismissed. As upsetting as it is, I hope it will provide a lead."

"Thank you, sir. I'll keep you informed." Standing,

he nodded his goodbye and left. Phelps's background told a terrible story, but he had an instinct that this might be the clue they had been searching for that would break the case wide open.

On his return to the office, Sanchez was waiting, tapping her foot and pointing to her watch. "Slow poke. That's not like you. You're never late."

"I was with the commissioner." He filled her in on everything he'd learned.

"About damn time. Does it smell like a good lead?"

She always teased him about being a bloodhound, slow and steady, sniffing the air for clues. It made an accurate analogy for the typical progress of an investigation. "It smells like the break we've been waiting for. All the pieces seem to fit, at least at this initial stage."

He poured them both mugs of coffee, passed her one, and sat down at his computer. "Let's have a look at the inheritance stuff first." They located the name of the attorney of record, Aaron Stills, who had dispersed Phelps's estate. After battling his guard-dog secretary, they threw their weight around a little to get him on the phone, on speaker.

Initially resistant to give them the details, he finally softened. "I guess it doesn't matter now. A lot of years have passed. The ten-million-dollar estate all went to his natural daughter. He never bothered to adopt her. Her name is Cara Belton."

He and Sanchez stared at each other in shock. *Finally, a break. A big one.*

"Hello…"

"Thank you for the information," Elijah said.

"Have you seen Ms. Belton at any time since she received the money?"

"No. There was no reason to keep in touch. I offered her legal assistance if she ever needed it, but she never took me up on it."

"I assume that means you don't have a current address for her?"

"I'm afraid not." They thanked him for his time and assistance. Elijah hung up the phone.

"Hot damn. It's her," Sanchez said, one leg jostling up and down with excitement.

"Cara Belton...Cassandra Bell. She even used the same initials."

"Maybe she's not as smart as we think."

He shook his head. "I don't think that's true. I think she wants to be caught. She's leaving just enough of a trail to eventually lead us straight to her."

Sighing, she said, "From now on, let's refer to her as Cara. It's getting confusing."

They spent the rest of the day combing the Internet, trying to find out anything they could about Cara Belton. The resulting information, or lack of it, was frustrating. Shortly after inheriting at age twenty-six, she disappeared after selling the estate and all its contents to a family who still resided there. A financial search showed that, although half of her inheritance remained in a local bank, it hadn't been touched in all of the years since Phelps's demise. The rest had been taken in cash, much to the chagrin of the bank president who still held that position. Where Cara and the money had gone, nobody seemed to know.

It certainly explained why they couldn't find a paper trail after that date, not even credit card receipts, even after a lengthy search. You could live a long time on five million dollars in cash.

"I think we're going to discover that six years ago is when the string of killings really began. Perhaps she killed her father and that spawned the idea for her revenge plot. Or maybe her father's death was an accident, and in the two years it took to settle the estate and sell everything, she came up with the plan." He pushed back from the desk and rolled the kinks out of his neck. "I'd bet on the first scenario."

Sanchez's fingers tapped away on the keyboard, then she paused. "Wanna see the frickin' house she grew up in?"

"Sure." Standing, he walked over to her desk, peering over her shoulder. A huge, brick mansion stood behind ornate, wrought iron gates. The structure had to be seven or eight thousand square feet. "It looks more like an upper-class hotel than a home."

"Back then, it sold, fully furnished, for four million smackeroos. It's probably worth a lot more these days." She stretched arms and legs in every direction, like a starfish. "So, she had five million to live on with a lot more left in the bank. No wonder she likes the high life."

"Using cash only is what allowed her to avoid the authorities all this time."

"I guess so."

"What time is it?"

"Seven-thirty."

"Time to head home?"

"Yes."

"Ray's makin' me dinner. Do you believe it?"

Her incredulity made him smile. "What's so

strange about that?"

"Nothin', as long as he doesn't expect me to reciprocate."

"I'm sure he knows better by now. Your whole salary goes for buying take out."

They split off at the nearest corner street, heading in opposite directions, and he walked home. Like most New Yorkers, he walked wherever he could or used his work vehicle and saved his car for trips outside of the city or emergencies. Fighting for parking or paying a fortune for a spot just seemed like a waste of time and money. Besides, walking was the only exercise he had time for, given his typical workweek.

He made himself a turkey sandwich after he changed into sweatpants and a t-shirt, but then, distracted, forgot to eat the second half. When he realized it had dried out, he threw it away. He pulled his rare treat out of the cabinet, a bag of chips he munched on, savoring the salty flavor and the satisfying crunch.

What would it be like to grow up in that huge house with only a perverted father around? Her mother long dead, she would only have servants to keep her company. Had she found friends? Perhaps a sense of isolation had helped cause the catastrophic trajectory of her life.

She'd moved out the second her eighteenth birthday arrived and lived in an apartment without roommates. Had he left her alone then or continued to torment her?

Impossible to know.

Giving up his speculation for the night, he wandered to bed and climbed in, his neighbors' nightly squabble providing an odd sort of New York lullaby.

****

Cara paced back and forth in her apartment. The most recent murder had died out of the newspaper already with barely a mention now. How were the creeps of the world going to recognize a warning that their behavior might provoke retribution?

She recognized that good men existed, a rare few at least, but someone needed to clear out the refuse of the rapists and pedophiles, all of the men who refused to take no for an answer.

It often seemed like swimming against a rising tide of polluted backwash.

This had been her calling for six long years and the work exhausted her. Well, eight, really, if she counted the rather inspired death of daddy dearest. Maybe the time had come to telephone Elijah. He always distracted her in one way or another. She picked up her latest throwaway cellphone, stabbing out his number. It rang and rang. At first, she was depressed, thinking he might not answer, then she heard the reassuring click. "Detective Black."

"For a moment, I thought you might be with another woman. Should I be jealous?"

"No such luck." He sounded grumpy.

"You don't sound very happy. Did I wake you?"

"Yes, Cassandra. I think it's safe to assume most people are asleep at two a.m."

She glanced at the clock, surprised when it confirmed the time. "Oh, I didn't realize it was so late, actually. Sorry. I was busy thinking about old times."

"Were you? Having any regrets about killing your father?"

She laughed. "How odd. I just thought about him

yesterday."

"Why don't you tell me why you killed him? How did it happen?"

Oh, he wants to play that game, does he? To see what helpful information I'll let slip. That's just fine with me. "Well, it was quite a clever plan if I do say so myself." She settled back into her chair. "He picked me up close to his house on his way to work as I, coincidentally, just happened to stroll along the road near his estate. Of course, he wanted to take me back to that hellhole of a house to pursue his forbidden pleasures, but I convinced him to carry on and find a different spot."

"So, you baited him, on purpose."

"Of course."

"How did you start the fire?"

His remark stopped her in her tracks. Her pulse beat faster and sweat beaded her forehead as she struggled to keep her tone even. "How did you know it was a fire?"

"Because I know Tyler Phelps was your father. I know who you are, Cara."

She knew she should hang up, but couldn't force herself to do it. "You know nothing about my life."

"Then tell me. Tell me how you killed him."

She paused, trying to focus despite the pain creeping in. "He insisted I sit next to him as he drove, and he put his hand between my legs. That predictable—it's how I knew the plan would work. I simply waited until a sharp bend in the road and spilled the contents of my to-go cup on his lap. It was pure alcohol. Slapping his lit cigarette into the mix was all it took. Poof." She laughed, but the sound strangled in her throat. She wiped away the tears that had come out of nowhere to trail down her cheeks.

"Were you injured in the accident?"

The gentle caring in his question made her pause. Nobody had ever showed concern about her being hurt. *Nobody.* "I had lots of bruises, but, luckily, nothing else." She heard her shaky voice and the loss of control maddened her. "After escaping the wreckage, I listened to him scream my name and watched him burn. And you know what? I wasn't sorry. I'm still not sorry."

"He was a terrible man."

She sucked in a breath, wiping her face on her sleeve. "More like a twisted monster. No one was willing to save me, so I did. I saved me."

He struggled with finding the right words, trying to reach her. "Aren't you tired, Cara? Aren't you exhausted from trying to make those awful men pay for their despicable acts?"

His empathetic words seeped into her soul. She sighed. "You're right, I am tired. I need to sleep." Clicking off the phone, she curled into the curved cushions of the sofa, wrapping her arms around herself in a desperate search for consolation.

Chapter Fourteen

The next morning, he received a surprise call from Jake Fisher, the musclebound bouncer at the club. His rusty voice scraped over the phone. "Hey, man. Don't know if this has nothing to do with your case, but the memory just popped into my mind. Three years ago, some crazy bitch stabbed a man in that same hallway. Forgot all about it until last night."

He didn't remember the case. "Were they a couple?"

"Nah, I guess the guy was trying to rape this one girl and the other one broke it up with a well-placed slice to the nuts."

"Were the police called?"

"Yeah, but I think it was hushed up some. I guess the dude was the son of some local politician. Never heard much more about it."

"What happened to the woman who stabbed him?"

"Man, she was gone before anyone caught on to what happened. They never found her."

You could never tell where you might get a lead from. "Thanks, Jake. Appreciate it."

"No prob, bro."

He filled Sanchez in. "You're kidding," she said. "If it was her, she just improvised that one, I guess."

"It would explain how she knew about the layout of the club. Let's look up the report and see what it says."

The report frustrated them, because it was bare bones and mostly just told them what Jake already had. He called the attending officer and caught him at his desk. "Oh, yeah. I remember that one. She knifed him right in his gonads. He bled all over the damn place."

"The report's a little on the skimpy side."

He lowered his voice. "Yeah, we got some pressure from the powers above to hush it up. The victim had attacked some chick and the ballsy one intervened. The woman who did the deed screwed off. But the victim was connected, and we were told to make it go away. You know how that bullshit works."

He knew how it was, but he didn't have to like it. "Thanks for the information. Appreciate it." After ending the call, he took a minute to fill Sanchez in.

Next, the two of them sat down to listen to his recording of the previous night's phone call. "You're right," his partner said. "She's tired. Do you think she's going to quit? We may never find her if she does."

"I think she's taking a break, but that will at least give us a chance at catching her. If I play it right, I might be able to convince her to turn herself in."

"How did the guys upstairs take this?"

"They want her name and picture in the paper."

"And you don't agree."

He shook his head. "I think it increases the chances of someone bungling the arrest, don't you? Either that or we'll get a million calls from people swearing that they've seen her, just to try and claim the reward they'll offer. It's a waste of resources. And I think it will anger her."

"Why would she be angry? Doesn't she want

attention?"

"I would bet she sees her true identity as something to be kept between the three of us. I think she'll see me as a traitor if it gets out. And that means no more phone calls which have supplied several good clues."

"Well, if she doesn't commit another crime, that's good, but it also means we're left with what we've learned so far which ain't much."

"I know." He ran a hand through his hair, at the moment feeling ten years older than his age.

One of the younger detectives stuck his head through the doorway. "You might want to turn on the television. That asshole that's running for mayor is shooting off his mouth about your case."

Sanchez scurried to switch it on, locating a channel where the candidate was just being introduced. They listened, aghast, to his warped take on the situation. "This idea of handling a killer with kid gloves just because she's a woman would never happen with me in charge. She's a maniac. They put down mad dogs, don't they, or at least chain them up? It's time for the police department to stop twiddling their thumbs and do their job."

A newsman shouted from the middle of the crowd, "What would you do differently?" A question the candidate ignored.

He continued on. "People like the Rivertons"—he pointed to the parents of the last victim who stood to one side of him—"should not be kept out of the loop. They have a right to know who murdered their son."

The inciting language droned on. Elijah turned off the broadcast in disgust. "He won't answer the media questions because he can't. He's just using this as a platform to launch his campaign."

"Nothing new about that." She shrugged. "And what about the Rivertons, anyway? They're friends of the current mayor, aren't they?"

"I think they'll use anyone to try and get their way."

"You're going to get the call from above soon. That naggy chick that heads up the media department will insist we release what we have, whether we think it's advisable or not."

Her words were prophetic. Called to the office once again, he entered to find all of the big guns waiting for him. They allowed him to make his point, but, for once, he was immediately overruled. His lieutenant apologized for not taking his advice. "At this point, I just don't think we have any choice but to expose her and hope for the public's help."

He tried and failed to ignore a surge of cynicism. "I assume this came from the mayor's office."

The other man nodded. "Do you have real concerns about revealing her name?"

"Yes. I think it will push her into another murder. If we could devote a little more time to it, I think I might be able to talk her into giving herself up."

"Based on the call last night?"

"Yes." He ran over the details again and reiterated his reasons for delaying releasing her name. His argument was to no avail. Ordered to show up for a three o'clock media briefing, he wandered back to the office, for once feeling both exhausted and ineffective. "Want to grab an early lunch?"

"Sounds like a plan."

They just ventured as far as the Mexican place

down the block, huddling in a back booth in an attempt at privacy. Cheaply recorded music with a bad mix of brass assaulted their ears. Depressed at being overruled, he abandoned his usual diet for a huge plate of enchiladas.

"Comfort food?" she asked.

He grunted assent. Trying to focus on eating the meal didn't work. Halfway through, the normally appealing scent turned his stomach. He pushed the remainder across the table to her. "This political bullshit is the one thing I hate about the job. All the attempts to manipulate the media into a position that favors the bigshots."

"Your fault. You shouldn't have been born so purdy." She glanced at his face and stopped teasing. Finishing her plate, she started on his leftovers. "Maybe you can still convince Cara to turn herself in."

He shook his head. "She trusted me because, even though I knew who she is, I didn't tell the world. Now, dammit, the whole thing is going to explode into a hellish mess."

She paused, wiping her mouth with a paper napkin and leaving most of her lipstick behind. "I wish I could say you're wrong, but I've learned to trust your instincts on things like this. Let's hope we're both wrong."

They bided their time walking back, needing a break from the frantic pace of their investigation. Other pedestrians sped around them as part of the city's constant, hectic rhythm. They raised their voices to be heard over the sounds of passing traffic.

After their return, Elijah spent the minutes before the media appointment figuring out how to say as little as possible beyond divulging her name and providing her photograph. Making his way slowly to the interview room, he wished there were some way to avoid making this appearance, but even he had bosses to obey. There were so many other helpful things he could be doing, things that might reach that dark, needy place inside Cara.

He faced the raucous crowd with a sense of resignation. Was it just his imagination or did the reporters seem louder than normal? The lights made him want to squint, and the heat from them caused a thin layer of sweat to form under his jacket. *Great. Sweaty and frustrated. Could this day get any better?*

Beginning by covering the bare essentials of the case, he then opened it up to questions. The first person said, "Are you just telling us this now because of the interview with a certain mayoral candidate this morning?"

He struggled for patience in the face of her accusatory tone. "We are sharing this information now because it was just discovered late yesterday. Next question." He worked his way through the crowd, picking at random.

"Isn't it true that Ms. Belton's name was withheld because she is from an affluent family?"

A headache started throbbing, and he forced himself to focus. He wished he'd swallowed a few painkillers earlier as a preventative measure. "There are a number of affluent people involved in this case. Any details that have been withheld are treated that way in order to solve the case as quickly as possible."

"Are there more crimes that we don't know about yet?"

Probably the dumbest question ever. He answered, "It's possible."

"Is it true that she contacts you, personally, on a regular basis?" This came from a reporter from one of the majors.

Where did they get that information? He frowned. "No comment. I think we're done here. Thank you."

It took him thirty minutes to confer with his bosses and return to his office. In that short amount of time, the news had spread online. Sanchez showed him a headline from a third-rate local rag that read, "Detective Hottie and His Killer Girlfriend."

Drivel from social media—just one more vexing complication he didn't need. He called the detectives on this case, those that were on duty, into the office. Hardening his expression, he said, "If I find out who leaked the phone calls between the suspect and me to the press, there's going to be hell to pay. It had better not be one of you. That's all."

No one looked guilty, but who knew? They filed out, whispering to each other. He didn't care if they were pissed. He had enough on his plate without worrying about what the press might screw up.

****

Cara woke up angry after a restless night and remained that way all day. She felt as if she'd been thrown to the wolves, seeing photographs of herself plastered on every news screen around. *Betrayal.* That was the gnawing feeling that tore at her gut.

She thought Elijah was different. She was certain he understood her calling. He would regret playing games and pretending to care about her. She wasn't someone to be trifled with. Yanking the files over into her lap, she tore through them, searching for the most deserving.

But the most deserving of them all were already dead.

So, who should be next in this never-ending line of hers? Who would make the biggest splash?

Her glance landed on his face, and she knew. And how she looked forward to the looming sense of relief she'd feel after this next job was done. Her hands stopped shaking as certainty took over. It would be spectacular—her next crowning achievement. She envisioned it, and all of the pieces started coming together.

She'd always been the creative sort. Now, she was ready to devote herself to a whole new project.

****

Elijah and Sanchez sat talking together in the office, their voices lowered. "We have three days to get this wrapped up," he said. "The mayor is going to insist on a task force, maybe even the FBI, if we don't get it solved by then."

"So, he cares more about what people think than actually solving the case."

"Pretty much." It wasn't that task forces didn't work at times. They just tended to slow things down with too many disparate opinions.

"Well, I think I found the right Elyse, the one that's Cara's mother," Sanchez said. "Found her picture in the university yearbook. Elyse Belton Preninger. I guess an illegitimate kid didn't merit the family surname." She opened a file and showed him a picture of a tall, slender brunette. "Pretty, for sure, from a rich family. Exactly the type Phelps would have been trying to snag. She died of ovarian cancer. Not sure that gives us any helpful information."

"Anything we can discover about her past is another piece we can use to stop her."

At lunch, he called and left a message for Mary that he would have to cancel their weekend date because of the progress of the case. Promising to call her next week, he made a note to do so. He'd screwed up too many relationships letting time slide by until women got fed up with the demands of his career. Determined to do better, he was trying to make his personal life a priority, so that he wouldn't end up a cranky old bachelor, spending all of his nights alone.

He hoped she would understand.

Staring at the map of where all the crimes had taken place, he added a pin for the florist shop. They had sent a bulletin out to all of the nicer hotels and apartment buildings, hoping that she would stick to her lifestyle choices. At this point, unfortunately, she likely had begun hiding somewhere atypical for her. That made tracking her a lot more challenging.

Late afternoon, the downstairs desk clerk called and told him someone named Lulu wanted to talk to him. He almost said, "Who?" before he remembered the redheaded girl, one of Banks's victims he and Sanchez had spoken to on the street. "Send her up."

Coming up the stairs instead of the elevator, she looked around as if she were a child's toy with a spinning head. She smiled as she caught sight of him standing in the doorway. "Hey, Detective Black."

"Hey, Lulu. Everything okay?" He waved her inside the office.

She perched on the edge of his desk, swinging her

legs and biting the edge of her lip. "Yeah. I don't even know if this is important. It just kinda popped into my head. I thought I'd stop by and tell you."

"Okay."

"You know the lady you're lookin' for, the pretty one we saw in the hotel?"

"Yes."

"She had an old scar on the inside of one wrist."

Well, that was the first time anybody mentioned that. "Do you remember which wrist?"

She squinted her eyes. "Yeah, it'd be her left one, 'cause she had a glass in her right hand."

"Okay." He made a note on his pad. "Can you describe it?"

"I can do better than that." She pulled up the sleeve of her blue, cotton blouse and pointed to the inside of her wrist. He recognized an old, faint scar caused by the unmistakable line of a razor blade.

"I tried to slit my wrists when I was thirteen," she said, sighing. "Her scar looked exactly like mine. That's why I noticed it. I couldn't believe someone who looked like her did the same thing I did."

Elijah went back over the basics of what she'd seen, but she never wavered and he believed her. To thank her, he gave her twenty bucks to buy her and her buddy some lunch. She acted as if he'd given her a thousand dollars. Thanking him, she started out the door and then paused to turn back. "Hey, Detective Black?"

"Yes, Lulu."

"Can you tell Sanchez thanks for the suggestion about the clinic? Just tell her they took care of the problem."

"Sure, Lulu. I'll let her know."

After she left, he felt grateful for the information, but sad, too. The teen years were hard for everyone, but thinking about how bad Cara's life must have been, and Lulu's for that matter, prompted compassion. The suicide rates for abused teenagers were terrifying.

He spent the last part of the long day looking back at all the security footage they had of Cara. Unable to see the scar because she wore the same bracelet on that wrist in every shot, he gave up. Hard to tell if the jewelry was rhinestones or diamonds, but, knowing her, probably the latter. So, any time she expected to be seen, she wore it. Lulu had only caught a glimpse of the scar because Cara had expected to blend into the high-society crowd at the hotel.

Her wearing that bracelet is not an accident. The scar was the only identifying mark they knew of, so he appreciated Lulu's observant nature.

Sanchez headed out to meet Ray, but he stayed and mulled over the files, hoping for another break. At eleven, he gave up and headed home.

The next day, he and Sanchez decided to track down some of the straggling pieces of the case. They spent the morning visiting places which specialized in body art. That ranged everywhere from spotless places with excellent reputations to the dark and dingy back-alley holes. They figured, though, that Cassandra was more likely to frequent the former type, and they were right.

At the fourth place they visited, the artist said, "Oh, sure, I remember her. I did a quote about justice on one arm and her boyfriend's name on the other." He ran a hand through his shoulder-length hair, allowing his gold stud earring to show. "I offered her a good deal on a permanent tattoo, but she wasn't into it. She just wanted the temporary variety."

"What did she look like?"

He shrugged. "Tall, streaky blonde hair, jeans. A bangin' bod."

"Do you remember her name?"

"Nah. She paid in cash, so I gave her a discount."

Thanking him, they left. "She's like a friggin' chameleon," Sanchez commented.

"Yes. And the men are so busy looking at her body, they don't notice much else."

"Oh, yeah, that's a surprise."

Next, they headed for a few stores carrying devices that others might consider torture devices. For the sadism and masochism crowd, though, they were status quo. He and Sanchez didn't exactly fit in with their regular customers. The buyers observed them closely, their mistrust evident by how they sidled away. "They made you for a cop, and they're freakin' out," she whispered.

At their second stop, they found the type of device they suspected had been used in the Riverton case. Elijah winced at the sight of it, but Sanchez seemed fascinated. "I should buy one. If Ray gets out of line…snap!" She squeezed the hinge again and let it close. Her enthusiasm made him wince.

It was cheap, so he bought it to show the medical examiner, knowing he'd be interested.

Chapter Fifteen

Nobody ever considered that someone who looked like her could be a gate-crasher. The beefcake security hired for that night's event didn't give her a second glance. Not one that went above her neck anyway. Dressed in a sexy costume, she slipped past one party guest after another, admiring all of the ornate masks. The most vital rule of the club; masks must stay in place at all times with anonymity both essential and guaranteed. Choosing to wear one of the feline variety, she'd purchased it from a store which specialized in such things.

Following her quarry here once before, a week ago, she'd figured out the nature of his interests. She tracked him here earlier this evening, observing from a distance, not wanting to arrive at the same time.

The long line of gleaming luxury cars disgorged costumed creatures of every sort, clad in myriad colors of silk, feathers and leather. It proved unnecessary to have a closeup view of the target's costume. After checking every exit, she concluded that it wasn't nearly as secure as they would have you believe.

Places like this were for men and women alike who had too much money to spend. Everyday things bored them, so they indulged in extremes of every variety. And, despite the misleading exterior, this was where they would find them, in a place not for the faint of heart.

Hadn't these people ever heard of sexually transmitted diseases?

She planned to watch the kinky bastards and bitches. Not much risk in that. A few might think it odd, but oddities were commonplace here. It's unlikely she would be the only voyeur.

Searching for just one man proved easy when you knew how to identify him. Neither his very proper wife nor his elegant mistress knew he attended these parties. It seemed quite apparent they would not approve.

But they would know by tomorrow. And so would everyone in New York.

It would be a two-phase attack if it played out the way she hoped, adding insult to grievous injury. An excruciating death paired with national exposure of the naughtiest kind—who could ask for more? The coverage would guarantee that her crimes held the front page for a few days at the very least.

She strolled into the open area just beyond the entry. The deviant devils within made a mockery of the elegant interior. A man dressed all in black, his red mask making him look like Lucifer, sidled up to her. "What do you have on under that dress?" he hissed, sounding like a second-string character from a porn flick.

"Absolutely nothing," she answered truthfully, ignoring his pathetic antics as she continued to stroll. A peculiar mix of leather, sweat and sex scented the air, colliding with expensive perfume for good measure. You couldn't bottle that, she thought, subduing a chuckle. If you could, these idiots would probably buy it in gallon drums.

As time ticked on, couples and threesomes indulged in all manner of excess. She glanced at them, absorbing their shrieks of delight, and moved on. It proved hard not to giggle, to be honest. Impossible to believe that they took all of this theatrical nonsense so seriously.

But how could she chastise them when she enjoyed her own costumes so much? Pondering that truth, she wandered down the stairs, locating him at last.

Her target lay secured to one of the beds in the open rooms downstairs, like a spider trapped of his own volition in a web of ecstasy. Surrounded by both men and women, he was dressed, head to toe, in thick straps of leather that exposed various body parts in a way that encouraged fondling.

Entitled to his taste in sexual excess, his crime lay in the fact that he had subjected some unwilling women to his cause. And waltzed away with a slap on the hand. No wonder, when so many judges assigned to these cases were men.

He thought he'd been oh, so careful now, joining these clubs which guaranteed anonymity. His error lay in forgetting he had a large, purple birthmark on the bottom of one foot.

When you were barefoot, identification was as simple as that. Magazine articles really did provide the strangest information these days. All it took was a bit of research to determine a weak spot. Once again, being well-read and observant had served her well.

As she watched, he groaned in ecstasy around the ball gag in his mouth as the onlookers took turns whipping him. The time came when he begged, his voice muffled, for a drink. That was her cue. She slid in between his over-stimulated observers and offered to deliver his glass of scotch, allowing them to continue their fun. Patting his leg, she slipped her note inside his outfit.

They were grateful and so was she. Gliding over to the long, well-stocked bar set against one wall gave her the opportunity to get his drink. She then ducked into a darker corner to tip the overdose of male stimulant into it and stir with her finger. Returning to his bedside, she delivered it to one of his playmates. The micro camera in her glasses continued to film as the woman helped him drink his liquor. Replacing his gag, he settled back and their activities resumed. Cara made sure to get a clear shot of the bottom of his feet with the oddly shaped mark.

When he started to perspire a little too much, she moved closer, fascinated. The overzealous crowd ignored her, shouting and offering encouragement to the man in the bed. He moaned louder and strained against the ropes. They only cheered his response.

He'd likely been given a safety word, as was typical, but they couldn't hear him over the surrounding clamor. She leaned close to one of the players. Raising her voice to be heard over the din, she said, "This is what he wants," slipping a broad elastic penis cuff into his hands. The man applied it, shouting encouragement as the victim writhed in pain.

She would have loved to have stayed to witness his demise, but she couldn't afford more risk than she had already taken. Only she knew that the overdose of enhancement along with the drugs for his heart would collide in a few moments and kill him. Or at least, that was the plan. She always had a plan B if it failed.

Hospitals were easy access for a sorceress like her.

On the thirty-minute drive home, she removed the tiny disc from her glasses and dropped it off with the security guard of a major network. Along with it, she provided a detailed note about the contents they would find on the footage including the person involved and the address of the party house. She marked the package urgent and told him they would certainly want to air it on the morning news. Since it involved a business competitor, she expected the response to be rapid and gleeful in terms of coverage. A certain segment of society loved to put people up on a pedestal, then relish tearing it down.

On arriving home, she shed her fanciful costume and donned a soft nightgown. Scrubbing her makeup off seemed to take forever, taunting her thinly disguised impatience. The news coverage in the morning would be more than she could ever hope to garner.

Unable to sleep, she paced around her dimly lit apartment, waiting for the sun to rise. Listening to Elijah's phone message again made her scoff. There wouldn't be another date. He could just go to hell where all the traitors of the world congregated.

When dawn finally broke, she switched on the television, flipping from channel to channel with a manic energy she couldn't contain.

Nothing.

Sitting down, she began to tremble. What could possibly have gone wrong?

Running the details of the operation over and over again in her head, she paused when the newsman interrupted his spiel. When she heard her victim's name, she ran to turn up the volume.

Not dead.
In the hospital.
Critical.

She sat down before her shaky legs buckled. Sucking in air, she struggled to think. She'd made a terrible mistake, changing her tried and true plans just to shake up the status quo. An ability to kill quickly was a source of pride for her. Her temper had got the better of her, and now, she had to practice damage containment.

Forcing herself, she focused on whatever information the newsman was adding. The words sex, scandal and forbidden were bandied around like so much cheap candy. They showed pictures of news crews and police milling around the party house.

Even if Pike survived, his life, as he knew it, would be over. Wasn't ruination the main point?

And then she remembered the note she'd slipped under the straps of his leather costume when she delivered his drink. She couldn't just pretend it was sexual shenanigans gone wrong now. It had her stamp on it.

What should I do?

For once, she didn't have an answer.

****

Elijah had been working at his desk since just after sunrise, checking paperwork from the previous day. The door burst open, startling him. Sanchez came racing in, stopping to drop her purse onto her chair. "Why aren't you watching the morning news?"

"Why would I?"

"Because," she said, hustling over to turn it on, "there's a lot going on compared to normal." Changing channels helped her find what she wanted. "Here it is. Get a load of this."

He listened, surprised to hear that Harrison Pike, the owner of one of the largest television networks in the world, had been injured at a party house. The big revelation that apparently fascinated his partner was that the location hosted parties interested in bondage games and swingers. He had been rushed to the hospital for unspecified emergency treatment.

Shrugging, he said, "Takes all kinds, I guess."

"You don't get it." She lowered her voice. "You know my girlfriend who's an EMT? She was on the ambulance call that went and retrieved him."

"That must have been interesting."

"You don't know the half of it." She smothered a giggle. "When officers and an ambulance responded to the house, the guests were either naked or in leather, whips and chains. A bunch of them tried to sneak out the back door. They all wore masks and our guys forced them to take them off. I guess there were politicians, actors, all kinds of famous people."

"I always figured the vice cops just looked the other way on that kind of thing."

"They do, but I guess someone dropped a recording off at a rival network during the night. There Pike was, in all his splendor, being whipped, with bulging parts in full view for everyone to admire. Isn't that somethin'?"

He poured himself a cup of coffee. "Oh, it's something, I'm sure, but I'm not sure it has much to do with us."

"Geez, c'mon. It's gotta make you laugh."

Not really. The whole pathetic mess depressed him, but he didn't want to come off like a judgmental parent.

"How serious are his injuries?"

"He's in critical condition."

That stopped him short. "You're joking. What did they beat him with? A baseball bat?"

She shook her head. "Apparently, it's his heart. I guess he has a pre-existing condition. They think the excitement gave him a heart attack. He coded on the way to the hospital, but they used the defibrillator and got him back."

"He may want to re-think his hobbies."

'You're tellin' me. Ain't no orgasm in the world worth dyin' for."

They worked in the office until late afternoon when the phone rang. It was one of the vice squad detectives. He requested they pay him a visit at the local hospital where Pike was a patient.

"Now?" Sanchez asked, frowning.

"Apparently, it's urgent and he doesn't want to talk to us over the phone."

On their arrival, Detective Jeff Campbell, as bald and skinny as new pencil, waved them into to an office and shut the door. "We got a new lead on this party-house deal that might have a tie-in to your murder case."

"How so?" Elijah asked.

"It looked originally like it might have been just sex games gone bad, but then we found this stuck to the inside of his outfit. It's already been dusted. No prints." He handed him a folded piece of paper.

Opening it, he read, "Violence is not the problem, it is a consequence of the problem."

"Do you know whose quote that is?"

He shook his head and looked it up on his phone.

"Someone named Jim Wallis."

"I know you found a folded note at one of your scenes. One of our newly transferred detectives told me so this morning. He said I should contact you two."

"We appreciate it." He paused, thinking. "Was there anything else about the scene that would lead you to believe it might be an attempted murder?"

"The only information we found curious is that his blood tests show an exceptionally high amount of male sexual enhancement drugs in his system. You may think that would be expected under the circumstances, but, apparently, he never used the things because of his heart condition. It was the one thing his wife and mistress agreed on." He tried, and failed, to stifle an inappropriate grin. "His...ah...member was so engorged, it took the nursing staff hours to coax it down. And, when he first arrived, he had an elastic cuff so tight around it that it's a wonder it didn't snap off."

"Do you mean his parts or the band?" Sanchez joked.

"Either." He cleared his throat, forcing his expression to seriousness. "Anyway, thought I'd better let you know asap."

"I appreciate it." Elijah stuck out his hand and shook. Sanchez followed suit. "While you're investigating, if you hear anything about a woman who took a particular interest in him, I'd appreciate you letting us know. Because of the note, I'm not sure if it was a failed attempt on his life or not."

"Will do."

They discussed the possible scenarios all of the way back to the office and couldn't come up with any solid conclusions. It seemed like a lot of trouble to go to just to humiliate someone. They would just have to see what else the investigation turned up.

Could it be a copycat? Unlikely, since the quotes had never been revealed to the public. And why another change in her modus operandi?

Later, at home, Elijah wondered why Mary hadn't returned his call. Had he messed up this connection already?

Chapter Sixteen

Cara learned late that night that her most recent target was expected to live. She had caused him enormous harm, but still, it had to be faced.

She had failed.

Failed for the first time in this long journey.

She felt like she had an anchor strapped to what remained of her heart. Offering an apology to whatever gods actually existed seemed appropriate, but what form should it take?"

Thinking in circles for half the night, she gave up in exhaustion, crawling into bed. One final solution intruded.

Maybe she should be the final sacrifice, in an attempt to atone for this latest fumbling attempt. Maybe she should just turn herself in to Elijah and be done with it.

****

A note with a message to call Detective Campbell lay on Elijah's desk the next morning when he arrived. The surge of energy he'd experienced on rising must have been a good omen. He picked up the phone, reaching the other man on the first try.

"Hey, thanks for getting back to me," Campbell said. "We got something from a witness last night I thought you might want to hear. Apparently, a female guest fetched Mr. Pike a scotch from the bar while he was enjoying himself. Nobody remembered noticing her before that point."

"Do you have a description?"

"Yes." He laughed. "She was dressed up as a cat."

"A cat?"

"Well, you know these folks like to wear masks, right? So, this chick is all dressed all in black except for a turquoise cat mask and long purple hair. She even had a tail. I guess she offered to bring the victim a drink, then stayed for a while to watch the show. Beyond a basic description, the only other comment most witnesses offered was that she had, and I quote, 'a body most men dream about.'"

"Was she still on site when you guys arrived?"

"Nope. We checked the witness statements and asked every cop on scene to be certain. Sounds like her errand offered plenty of time and opportunity for her to add those pills to his drink, though. She was able to walk across the room and back with no one paying any attention to her other than noticing her curves."

Thanking him, he hung up. This crime seemed all over the place to him, disorganized and poorly planned. But still, she hadn't left them much to work with.

Was she devolving?

He and Sanchez took turns later that afternoon filling in the lieutenant on the progress of the case. Elijah suggested that they might want to put a guard at Pike's hospital room now that he appeared to be improving. They were interrupted by the phone ringing. The lieutenant answered it, spoke in low tones, then hung up. "Pike just died. His heart packed it in."

Elijah sat without speaking, his mind racing. "Is there any way we can keep this news from the media?"

His lieutenant looked perplexed. "Why would you want to?"

"If our killer thinks he's still alive, she might be tempted into making another play for him."

He paused, considering. "It's a bit risky, setting a trap with so many other people around."

"True, but it might be our only chance to stop her before she kills again."

They weighed the pros and cons, deciding to move forward with the plan. The lieutenant said, "Let me head over to the hospital and explain the plan to the family. We'll only have a day or so to try this, you two. The manpower costs are too high to carry it on any longer."

They nodded. "We'll start working on the details immediately." Later, they were called into the commissioner's office to explain the basics of their plan. Between keeping the hospital staff safe and setting up a fake victim, it wouldn't be easy.

"Are you thinking she might make another attempt?"

"Yes. He's the only victim who she thinks has survived. She's losing control. I think she'll see it as a failure."

"That makes sense. I'll allow the extra manpower." He sat back, meeting Elijah's gaze. "Tell me how you want to proceed."

He agreed with the basic outline of their plans and dismissed them. Walking back to their office, Sanchez poked him in the arm. "We both know you're the strategy guy. I'm the muscle." She popped a rather impressive bicep, grinning. "Let me know about whatever game plan you come up with. I'll be ready to go first thing."

He remained at the office until midnight, poring over all of the case files and considering every possible scenario. There could be no slipups. If only Cassandra would call...but instinct told him he'd heard the last word from her.

The late Harrison Pike was the only bait they had. They could protect the hospital better than they could a lot of places. But if it went wrong, it could go terribly wrong, putting dozens of people at risk. With a larger operation, one person could screw up and cause all their hard work to all come crashing down. He switched off the desk light and decided a few decent hours of sleep would be beneficial if he could manage it. On a whim, he swung by Mary's rental on the way home, standing on the street in front like a lovestruck boy.

Why hadn't she called him back? Continuing towards home, he decided he'd drop by in the morning and try to catch her before work. Feeling better with a skeleton plan in place, he went back to his house to get some sleep.

In the morning, well rested for a change, he left his house thirty minutes early to try and catch Mary before she left for work. He dodged around the morning traffic and all the kids, chattering and laughing, on their way to school.

When he turned into the corner of her street, he stopped, staring. A middle-aged man in baggy work clothes stood in the front yard of her place, pounding a For Rent sign into the lawn.

He lengthened his stride to catch him before he had a chance to leave. "Excuse me. Do you have more than one rental in that house?"

Shaking his head, he answered, "No. I live in the basement and rent out the top floors, but it's small, so it's only one unit." He gave the sign a final tap. "Why? You interested?"

"No. I live around the corner. I was wondering what happened to your tenant."

"The teacher?"

"Yes."

He narrowed his gaze, growing suspicious. "Who wants to know?"

"I'm a friend." He introduced himself and pulled out his badge to put the landlord's mind at ease.

"She's not in some kind of trouble, is she? She was an excellent tenant. To tell you the truth, I was kinda hopin' to keep her around a little longer."

"No. She's fine. I just didn't know she planned to move."

"Me, either. She just knocked on my door yesterday and said she had a sudden change in plans. I can't complain because she paid me an extra month for the bother. Best part is, she did a real good job of cleanin' up, so I can rent it right away."

Thanking him, he headed back down the road, puzzled. He hoped nothing had happened to cause her sudden change of plans. Mary had no family, though, so what could have prompted a move?

On impulse, he turned right instead of left, texting Sanchez that he would be a few minutes late for work as he walked. The school was only four blocks away. It might be a little awkward for him to show up unexpectedly at her workplace, but he wanted to make sure she was okay.

Groups of kids were walking and talking in the

sprawling school yard, a few playing catch for the last few minutes before the school bell rang. Although he could spot a few teachers milling in the yard, he couldn't see Mary. He walked up to one of the women who stood, watching the kids, her red coat highlighted by a graffiti-covered wall behind her. "Do you know where I can find Mary Brown?"

"Teacher or student?" the woman asked, laughing. "We have both with that name."

"Teacher."

She pointed to the front entrance of the school. "She'll probably be in her classroom. Third door on the left."

He entered the crowded building, dodging groups of chattering kids, hoping she wouldn't be upset at the interruption. When he poked his head through the doorway, an older woman was hanging a large, framed world map and he sighed. *Where is she?* "Excuse me, ma'am. Would you happen to know where I can find Mary Brown?"

She turned with a welcoming smile, tucking a stray gray hair behind one ear. "I'm Mary Brown. How can I help you?"

His mind stuttered, then took hold. "Do you teach grade three?"

"Yes. For the last fifteen years. Are you a parent?"

"No." Walking across the room, he pulled out his badge and held it up for her to check. "I just had a question for you. Has there ever been another Mary Brown who worked here? In her thirties, slender, brunette?"

"Not in the last fifteen years, at least. And I would know. We're a pretty tightknit bunch."

In a daze, he thanked her for her time and left the school grounds. He walked in the direction of the precinct. His normally disciplined brain ran like an out-of-control train, crashing into its linear destination.

Was he crazy?

He started to think about the odd timing of her retreat.

Running into Mary at the bar, a book on philosophy in her hand.

Her turning down his offer of dinner on the night Matthias Riverton was killed.

Her lack of reaction when he mentioned the kids at her school.

Nobody was that good an actor.

Nobody.

And yet...

He sped up, weaving around other pedestrians on the sidewalk. Ignoring the crowded elevator to vault up the stairs when he finally arrived at the precinct, his heart rate pounded in premonition.

Sanchez tried to speak to him as he entered the office. He waved her aside, grabbing the file of photographs they'd taken off the footage obtained from the Banks' tapes. He flipped through them, looking to compare them with the one good photograph of Cara Belton from years ago and his memory of Mary's face.

And there it was. He plucked it from the pile and stared.

Was he imaging things?

No, even though she'd only been a teenager, it was there in the shape of her eyes, the contour of her nose.

Sanchez grabbed his arm. "What's wrong?"

He shoved the photograph in front of her. "Who is

this?"

She squinted. "This could be one of Cara Belton, right?"

"Who else?"

"What do you mean, who else?" She pulled up a chair, shoving him into it. "Did you get any sleep last night?"

He told her what had happened on his way to work. "I think that Cassandra, Cara and Mary are all the same person."

"Nah, you're crazy. Mary's too short and, sorry, but not nearly as pretty."

"But think about it." He struggled to be objective. "Cara wore very high heels at every crime scene. And Mary didn't wear any makeup and she had glasses. Both would really change her look. So would tinted contacts and a wig."

"Their voices are different."

"It's not that hard to change the pitch of your voice."

"Maybe." She tapped her nails on the desktop. "Is it the timing you're thinking about?"

"Yes. That's why she always knew where we were. She had all day to follow us and, half of the time, I told her where I'd be."

"If it's her, do you think she made a run for it?"

He shook his head. "No. I think she's somewhere right in the thick of it, waiting to make her next move."

"But where?"

"Great question. I wish I had an answer." He stood and poured himself a cup of coffee, topping off Sanchez's. "I think abandoning her apartment means she's heading for some kind of grand finale. I might be wrong, but, if I'm right, we need to put our plan in place right away."

****

Cara toasted the elegant blonde who peered back at her via the reflection in the floor to ceiling windows. She looked positively scrumptious again. It wasn't vain to state the obvious, was it? Donning fashionable clothes and a great wig was like getting a transfusion of blood when your body craved replenishment.

Of all the places Elijah and Sanchez might look, they would never believe she would come back here, where she'd slaughtered the commissioner's brother. Simply picturing his bloody, rotting corpse warmed her cynical heart. It had been like killing her father all over again, the comparison supplying endless delight.

The crime scene had finally been released by the police. After that, the resulting mess had been cleaned up by professionals who specialized in that kind of work. Scrubbing away blood and gore for a living—she couldn't imagine it. Strolling around, inspecting the apartment, she gave them a grudging B plus.

The sprawling suite didn't need to be pristine, just worthy of her presence. It's not like she would sleep in that dreadful bedroom anyway. It looked like exactly what it had been: a middle-aged man's version of a sex den. Now that the filthy bastard was dead, the apartment would sit empty until the beneficiaries got around to putting it on the market. Sooner or later, some other social climber would buy it to celebrate an empty life.

That would take a while. She'd provided the commissioner and his peons with lots of puzzle pieces to keep them occupied.

The one decision she struggled with involved which drama to create for her grand finale. Did she want to kill Harrison Pike as he lay in a hospital room, helpless? She'd watched all of the extra activity surrounding the place and guessed what the police had planned. Elijah was getting desperate.

It didn't seem like enough of a challenge for her. She'd always been easily bored. Surely Pike had taken up enough of her precious time already.

Whatever she chose, would she invite Elijah to her coup de gràce? She didn't feel quite as angry at him now that she'd freshened up. Failing to realize the mousy brown hair and that dreadful apartment depressed her too much had almost been a fatal mistake.

Maybe she was just a teeny bit vain.

She wished now that she had vamped Elijah as her current character, the delicious Cassandra Bell. If she had done so, would he have even glanced in her direction?

Probably not. After all, he'd been attracted to the plainest jane of all her personalities. *Such a fascinating man.*

Had she met him in another life, she might have chosen him as her mate, vanquishing him in bed as the polar opposite of the very boring Mary Brown.

But she wouldn't be granted another life, would she? Despite her last costume, she wasn't a cat, so she had no nine lives that allowed another do-over. Pain tightened her chest. Wandering over to pour herself another glass of wine, she settled in a chair to watch the clouds drift overtop the highest buildings.

Chapter Seventeen

Elijah's convoluted plan slipped into place. In as low key a way as possible, an undercover cop impersonating Harrison Pike had taken his place in his hospital room. They'd even managed to find a policewoman who looked similar to his wife to come and go as the real woman had been doing. A rotating group of police officers remained to guard the door. They were under orders to allow themselves to be lured away under the right circumstances.

Elijah stood with Sanchez, waiting to take part in another dreaded press conference, one designed to coax Cara out of hiding. They had planted questions with a few trusted news people, all manufactured to goad her. Whether it would work or not was anybody's guess. It simply represented their best shot at being able to direct and control the action of the takedown in a safe manner.

Showtime. After being introduced, he stepped forward and said, "I have a statement, after which I will take just a few quick questions. As all of you know, the assault on Harrison Pike was rumored to be a failed attempt by serial killer Cara Belton. We discovered this morning that this theory is not correct. Mr. Pike was, in fact, drugged by a former employee attempting to get back at his employer. He tried to copy Ms. Belton in order to avoid detection. Mr. Pike is recovering nicely, and we expect him to be released in the near future.

Any questions?"

"How did you discover it was a hoax?"

"We were suspicious from the very beginning because the crime was so sloppy compared to the others. I doubt Ms. Belton would have left him alive. She would have seen that as a failure and done something about it."

"Will Mr. Pike have protection to ensure against a second attack?"

"Mr. Pike will continue to be under the protection of the NYPD until further notice."

"Has Ms. Belton contacted you again?

"Any contact has ceased, and I don't anticipate hearing from her again. That's it for today. Thank you."

He and Sanchez returned to their office. All of the questions had been designed to provoke some kind of action, hopefully in a place they could control. Only time would tell if their plan to capture Cara worked. Back in the office, Elijah slumped in his chair as Sanchez perched on the edge of the cluttered desk. "You seem a little depressed, pal. Are you okay?"

"Well, considering I had a date with a serial killer and didn't even know it, I'm on the top of the world."

"Feelin' like a dumbass?"

"That's an understatement."

"Well, snap out of it. I mean, it's not like schmoozing women is your specialty."

"You're not helping me feel better about my abilities in detection or seduction."

She leaned over to mess up his hair. "Oh, come on. Chill. I just mean you can't have it all. You got looks, brains and you're actually a nice guy, which, believe me, is a rarity in this world. If you had game with the ladies, too, it would just be overkill."

He recognized it was her way of cheering him up. "Thanks."

"Do you really think she'll make a try for Pike? Well, you know what I mean. The Pike substitute?"

"I'm not sure. I'd say it's a fifty-fifty chance at this point. It's all we've got."

"You don't think she'll go after you, do you?"

"No."

"You can't be certain, you know. She's changed directions a few times already."

"What, now you're worried?"

She rolled her eyes. "Yeah. I don't want to waste time breaking in a new partner."

They continued working, feeling like mice on an exercise wheel. Hours later, after Sanchez had long gone, he forced himself back into that small room to search the DVDs. Instinct warned him what he was going to find hidden somewhere in the ones he had left. A sense of foreboding bore an acid-driven hole in his stomach.

A few minutes past midnight, he located the previously unseen footage he'd been dreading. Cara's face still had the baby fat that marked her as an early teen. Her expression, wildly terrified at first, changed to dazed after Phelps forced her to drink a glass full of liquid. "You'll feel so good," he crooned, tipping it down her throat.

In minutes, he had her sit on a chair as he pulled off her dress, turning to leer at the camera. Her naked body was still that of a child. He groped her breast, and even drugged, she tried to pull away, whimpering. He forced her to spread her legs and turned back to the camera. "Close up." The camera zoomed in and then back out.

He straightened and began pulling off his clothes, insisting she watch. When his engorged penis came into view, she began to sob in choked coughs. The monster turned back to the camera and grinned. "Hey, Ed, watch me make a baby with my baby." He turned and moved toward her.

Elijah ran for the bathroom, barely making it to the toilet before his stomach erupted. His knees on the hard, tiled floor, he held on to the rim as if it was a float that kept him from sinking.

He understood Cara's tragic life, now, in a way he hadn't before.

He understood the torturous rage that powered the destruction of her burning soul. The fury that refused to die.

Had he been there at the roadside all those years ago, he knew that he, too, would have stood by and let this evil man burn.

****

Sloppy, Cara thought, her temper soaring. She slapped her glass of wine down on the coffee table and the stem snapped, slicing her hand. Her reaction sent red wine gushing over the cream carpet. Elijah told everyone the crime was sloppy, did he? And now, she wouldn't even get the credit for exposing Harrison Pike as a pervert.

Elijah was becoming an endless nightmare instead of the man of her dreams.

She stormed over to the porcelain kitchen sink to rinse the blood off her hand. The mere sight of it calmed her as it dripped into the sink, leaving red rivulets to stain the pristine surface.

It was vital to remember who she was dealing with: the brilliant Elijah Black. *So, so smart*. Almost as smart as everyone thought. She laughed, sudden relief flooding through her. It uplifted her to see through his machinations. Did he really think it would prove that easy to manipulate her? *Fat chance.*

She wondered if he'd paused his investigation long enough to notice she had disappeared from both her pathetic abode and his life. *Had he even tried to see her?* Brushing rebellious tears away, she reassured herself that she no longer cared what he did.

"You want to play, Elijah?" she murmured to herself. "Let's play." Grabbing a small cotton towel from the linen closet, she wrapped it around her hand to stem the bleeding and began to plan the ultimate finale.

****

Elijah and Sanchez studied every area of the various hospital entrances over and over again, hoping to cover every possible scenario Cara could cook up. No one would be in the rooms on either side of their bait's location to give them an extra safe zone if she made the attempt on his life. Only a restricted number of staff was being utilized, and they were well-informed about what was going on in their ward. The other nursing staff and patients had been transferred to another floor until the threat passed.

Copies of every available photograph of Cara Belton, in all of her incarnations, had been provided to hospital security. The staff were on high alert. Extra plainclothes officers had been ordered to police the surrounding area until further notice.

The hospital had provided a Spartan office for the

partners to work from, and in it, Elijah paced back and forth between the utilitarian desk and the door. "We can't afford to miss one tiny detail, no matter how small. She'll take advantage of any oversight."

"It's all covered," Sanchez said. "You worry too much. We've gone over this stuff a dozen times."

"If there's a hole, she'll find it."

"C'mon. Let's go check the other buildings like you said. You'll feel better if you do."

When they were verifying all of the details, it had occurred to him to check all of the surrounding buildings because the top floors looked down on the hospital. He didn't think Cara would suddenly use sniper tactics—that was a stretch—but she could observe and gather information on who was where at what time, something at which she excelled.

They spent a few hours checking parking garages, dodging entering and exiting cars. They included roof-top terraces, etc., in their search but didn't find anything or see how she could discover something that could jeopardize their plans.

As they finished, Sanchez's stomach gurgled. "I need to get somethin' to eat."

"It's only…" He glanced at his watch. *Three o'clock. How did that happen?* "Sorry. I guess we missed our lunch."

"No time like the present." Taking the elevator back to street level, they found a convenient deli just a few storefronts away. He had no plans to eat, but she overrode his objections, buying him a pastrami sandwich and shoving him into a booth while she bought them colas. "Seriously, you're skinny enough without skipping meals."

He preferred to think of himself as fit but had to admit she might be right. He hadn't been eating enough lately. Forcing himself to take a bite, he found the next one came a little easier. "I can't help feeling that we're missing some essential detail."

"Jeez, it's not easy. This thing has too many tiny parts: the crimes from years ago, more recent ones, the current murders themselves. It's just hard to keep track of all the bad guys. We're doing the best we can, partner. It's all anybody can ask."

"If anybody else dies, it's on me."

"Ah, that's bullshit and you know it. The fault lies with the one who's doing the killing. And she's been doing this crap for years. You're not the only cop in town. Why didn't someone catch her before now?"

"I suppose." She seemed a little fidgety today, prompting him to ask, "How's Ray doing?"

Her fingers started tapping on the table, her trademark sign that something troubled her. "He's okay."

"Is everything still copacetic between you two?"

"I guess." She swallowed a swig of soda. "He's kinda tightening the lasso a little bit."

"How so?"

"You know, the whole 'let's have dinner together every night' kind of thing."

"And that's not what you want?"

She shrugged. "What do I know about all that happy-ever-after garbage? Jeez."

He was one of the few people who knew Sanchez had lived through a very violent childhood, then ended up as a teenager with a boyfriend who almost beat her to death. It was why she had become a cop and the reason she excelled at dealing with victims, but it had also left her with a massive problem trusting anyone.

"Want some advice?"

"You mean some skinny, white-man psycho-babble? Not really."

"I'm going to give it to you, anyway, because you're not just my partner, you're my friend. Just tell him you need to take it slow. You've seemed happier with him than you've been with anyone in all the years I've known you."

She listened to what he had to say, but reverted to jokes on the way back to the office, her way of changing the subject.

In the early hours of the next morning, when he should have been sleeping, he went over and over where Cara could have gone to hide. Contrary and dramatic, she would try to pick the least likely place he would look. Where would that be? He tried to think through a variety of options.

And, suddenly, with blinding clarity, he knew. The Edgar Banks scene had been cleared a few days ago. Would she really be that brazen? The possibility made his heartbeat thump in his chest. After grabbing a quick shower, he pulled on his clothes as quickly as he could, texting Sanchez so she would know where to find him.

He entered the building thirty minutes later, pausing to ask the night doorman if he'd seen anything. The man said no, but seemed too sleepy to have noticed much. He travelled up to the correct floor, unsnapping his holster to rest his hand there.

Creeping up the hall and inside, pistol at the ready, he found the apartment empty. It became clear after checking that she had been there, though, and very recently. The scene made it apparent, too, that things were falling apart for her. He worried about the sight of bloodstains until he found the shards of glass and could picture her temper tantrum. On the table she'd left a typed note. It said, "You're a day late and a dollar short, Elijah."

Oh, Cara. He probably shouldn't pity her, but knowing what he knew now, he did.

His musings were interrupted by Sanchez's arrival. She hailed him from the door so as not to surprise him, then entered, looking around. "Looks like you were right. Damn it." She put her hands on her hips. "Where do you think she's headed now? Any guesses?"

"Don't have a clue." He sighed. "I guess her showing up at the hospital is our best bet, now."

Chapter Eighteen

Cara wandered around Elijah's home, examining every minute detail with great interest. How could a policeman not have a security system? True, the locks had been harder to conquer than average, but she was very, very good at what she did. Her professional set of lock picks had been her pride and joy for years.

Quite astonishingly clean for a man, he had everything carefully tucked into a tidy corner. Even a plate and cup, likely from breakfast, had been washed and left to dry on a rack beside the spotless kitchen sink. The laundry baskets she found on the dryer made her giggle—boring, white plastic with "Clean" marked on one and "Dirty" on the other. After all, there was such a thing as being too practical.

The whole house was clearly a mix of his things and items his parents had left behind. More sentimental than she would have expected, he maintained a tidy table full of framed family pictures in the living room. Most were of the three of them, him and his parents, from baby pictures to photos of him in uniform as a young cadet. Probably the inherited collection of his doting mother.

He had been not just loved but cherished by these people. Cara felt a stab of unexpected jealousy. She barely remembered her mother, the tragic Elyse, although sometimes scenes would flit through her mind of her brushing her hair or picking out a dress. Having no idea if they were actual memories or something imagined to console herself, she didn't pay them much heed.

She wished she could forget her life from twelve to eighteen, but her father's ghost still chased her, unrelenting. His memory cornered her and pinned her down every time she took a step forward. The scent of his aftershave remained on her skin to this day, even after she scrubbed herself raw time after time in a futile effort to rid herself of his scent.

The night was her enemy, when tortured memories morphed into nightmares. The reason she meted out punishment during those hours was so that the recipient might end up as terrorized as she'd been, alone in the darkness.

She finally made her way up the steep, carpeted staircase to Elijah's bedroom, running her fingers along the gleaming wood bannisters. Stepping inside, she scanned the room. The same deliberate order lived here as well, although he had simply pulled up his covers when he exited the bed.

After removing her shoes, she smelled his clean, strong scent permeating the crisp linen sheets. Slipping between them, sighing, she decided to take a cat nap. He'd be at work for hours, but even if he caught her sleeping, would that be such a bad thing?

Waking twenty minutes later, she reluctantly left the shelter of his bed. She resumed her search and located his home office next door in one of the spare bedrooms. All manner of books crowded the cases on every wall: tomes on philosophy, of course, but also literature, history, psychology…There was even some erotica. Now, that was interesting. Did the perennial good boy have a naughty streak somewhere underneath that conservative shell? The possibility intrigued her.

The only other items in the room were a majestic antique desk, a matching chair and his desktop computer. She searched through the various drawers. Most were filled with the usual paraphernalia you would expect to find: pens, pencils and computer paper. In the bottom of the last drawer, however, lay a single intriguing item. The piece of linen stationary was heavy and expensive, the writing dark and flamboyant against the ivory background.

It read:

The nights are agony without you.

It was signed with an elegant, flowing letter L. The letter had a subtle scent, floral she thought, although it was faint. Who was this mystery woman who yearned for him?

It touched her, somehow, that he would secret this timeless treasure away and only look at it when he was alone. Instinct had her folding it to slip into her bra. She had wanted something personal of his and now she claimed it. His secret, their bond, to keep nestled close to her heart.

She would have loved to have grown up in a house like this where possessions actually had meaning and weren't just an abundant display. She didn't really own anything that had meaning. If she lost one thing, she simply replaced it with another.

The diamond bracelet she wore was a reminder of her vow, despite the fact that her father had given it to her as payment for services rendered. He'd said that, laughing, shortly before she killed him. It covered her scar perfectly, but glancing at it also strengthened her resolve to leave a trail of emasculated bodies in her wake. One payment for another, as it were. The glittering diamonds were a symbol for the entire bloody battle.

In her rush, she almost forgot to take a selfie as a memento. Sitting back down at his desk, she chose the bookcase as an appropriate background. She tilted her cellphone and smiled, taking several shots to be sure she had an acceptable one.

Glancing at her watch, she saw it read almost three o'clock. He'd be home in a few hours, maybe less when she sent the photograph.

Time to go. She cast one final, regretful look around. Treading carefully down the stairs, she made her way to the front door, opening it, then closing and locking it behind her.

****

Around four-thirty, Elijah heard the message alert ding on his cellphone and received the selfie. He stared at it, confused, as he recognized the background. Why in the hell had she gone to his house? Grabbing his coat, he said, "I have to check something out."

"Need help?" Sanchez asked from the seat at her desk.

"I'm good. Be back in an hour."

"Why don't you just head home early?"

"No, I'll spend tonight at the hospital."

Her eyebrows drew together. "Jeez, is that really necessary?"

"I think so."

"Okay. Better you than me."

He hurried home, his worried eyes checking out

every passing pedestrian on both sides of the road on the way. When he arrived, the locks on both front and back doors appeared intact. He entered slowly, panning his pistol right and left in a sweep. He didn't think she would shoot him, but he wasn't taking any chances. Checking the entire house didn't reveal any damage. He couldn't see that anything had been moved, taken or damaged. *Why in hell had she come here? Just to prove she could?*

His final run through revealed the only things that appeared to have been touched were his sheets. They looked more rumpled than when he'd left. A closer inspection showed that his pillow had been moved from his usual side. It reminded him of that old children's tale. *Who's been sleeping in my bed?*

Was she looking for comfort or calamity? He stared again at the selfie she'd sent him. At first glance, he would have said she seemed happy, but, on closer inspection, her smile appeared forced, not quite reaching her eyes. He returned downstairs to confirm everything looked normal. Double-checking all of the locks, he arrived back at the precinct just as Sanchez headed home.

"Everything okay?"

He pretended not to see her curious glance. "Sure. See you in the morning."

The frustrating night passed in a blur, to no avail. He sat, propped up in an uncomfortable chair with their "bait patient," but Cara didn't show. At some point, he started to realize that maybe he had figured this scenario all wrong.

But where would she go? Where else was left?

It annoyed him that he had lost control of the

investigation. They had been riding a downward curve since the press conference. It was getting harder and harder to put one foot in front of the other as inevitable exhaustion took its toll.

When he showed up at his precinct, his day-old clothes rumpled from his all-night sojourn, Sanchez pointed to the office door. "Go home. You need a shower and some sleep."

"I have to figure this out."

"Seriously, I have never seen you in rumpled clothes, ever, never mind the five o'clock shadow. That's not like you and it's freakin' me out."

"Cara was in my house yesterday."

That stopped her scolding rant. "What are you talking' about?"

He grabbed his phone and scrolled to the selfie, showing her.

She peered at it, shaking her head. "No wonder you're flipping' out. Why didn't you tell me?"

"I wanted to determine the reason she went there, but I didn't have much luck."

"Was anything missing?"

"No, but she climbed into my bed."

"What? Why would she do that?"

"I don't know." He huffed out a breath. "But it worries me that I'm not reading her right, because I never saw it coming."

"Jeez, pal, she's all over the place. The best shrink in the world couldn't follow her now, never mind us mere mortals."

He refused to go home, despite her cajoling, but grabbed a few hours' sleep in the off-duty room provided for such things. After a glance in the mirror, he decided to shower and shave. Dressing in the spare fresh clothes he kept in his office helped rejuvenate him. He still didn't feel encouraged by their sluggish progress on their case, but he at least felt more rested.

In discussions with the lieutenant, they decided to give the hospital scene one more night to make sure Cara wouldn't come, then shut it down. It was costing too much in terms of manpower to continue and the hospital board was complaining about the disruption of regular service.

****

Cara sat, observing, wondering how to best get close to her next target. Surrounded by people from morning to night, he couldn't be lured by her usual assets. He was in a hopelessly boring, long-term marriage to his ultraconservative wife. His crimes were linked to money, not sex.

Payoffs were the name of the game. A deep hack into his personal accounts showed massive deposits right after two of the three Tanner King cases were decided in his favor. It couldn't be coincidence. Nor were the vacation photographs afterwards that showed the two had become buddies, laughing it up at the expense of the victims.

But now, well, payback really was long overdue and would come calling any day now.

Sitting in the back row of the busy courtroom, she watched as the esteemed Judge Rutherford Hart brought down his wooden gavel with a bang. She trailed the rest of the spectators out. Wandering to the back entrance, she waited inside the doorway until she saw him stride, briefcase in hand, over to his shiny, black car: a top European make, of course.

No reason to follow. He'd do the same damn thing he did every day, head home to his society matron wife. Cara knew because she'd tailed him for the last three days. He lived a mere two streets away from the house she'd grown up in.

Apparently, money was his only noticeable vice. Other than that, he might make the top ten list of the most boring men she'd ever followed. Several naïve female victims had relied on him to render fair judgement and he had failed them, choosing accumulating material goods over administering justice. That couldn't be allowed.

If she knew anything about dynamite, she would simply blow that fancy car of his sky-high with him in it. She could consider it celebratory fireworks. But that wouldn't work. Too dangerous.

She carried the problem back with her to the shoddy little hotel room, mulling it over as she tried to ignore her depressing surroundings. How to kill the judge became an odd puzzle to solve. She'd run out of the paralytic drug she'd used in the other cases, and her source had disappeared back into the dark underground world of supply and demand.

Poison was always easy, but it would be difficult to get that close to him without being noticed. Shooting him had to be considered as an option, but it didn't seem poetic in nature. His death should have that necessary touch of drama.

It had to be perfect because she'd screwed up the last one. This one had to succeed at all costs.

****

The following day, Elijah had to admit the intricate hospital trap had been a resounding failure. He and

Sanchez spent the morning cancelling all the extra patrols and apologizing to hotel administrators for the unnecessary disruption.

In the afternoon, he gave a rather depressing news conference explaining the reason for the subterfuge and breaking the news about Pike's death. All the news people wanted to know about was how they were going to proceed with the investigation. *Damn good question.* He wondered what they'd do if he just told them the truth and admitted he didn't have a clue.

The hard truth of it was that he hadn't yet determined an answer, but he offered the usual platitudes and ended the question period. Afterwards, he heard that Pike's family had caused a scene in the commissioner's office, complaining bitterly about their father's killer still not having been caught.

A pounding headache chased him all day and he went home before supper, a rarity. After taking some painkillers, he crawled into bed without eating. A while later, he fell into a restless sleep full of frustrating dreams.

Chapter Nineteen

An extra day spent following Judge Hart had finally provided Cara with an interesting tidbit. She'd heard the bailiff discussing growing flowers with him. Apparently, the judge's habit was to spend an hour after work alone in his rose garden, tending the buds, his wife strictly forbidden to join him. He had laughed about it being his single hour of solitude.

This small window of opportunity provided Cara with enough time to carry out her plan. With the use of binoculars, the garden at the back of the house could easily be seen. Access was uncomplicated. Mature trees offered plenty of shelter in other parts of the lawn. There were no security cameras outside either, just a brick and wrought-iron wall that would be easy to scale.

And the weapon? Well, it would have been great fun to see the look on Elijah's face when he heard what she'd used. Even he would have to be impressed.

She spent the rest of the busy day preparing for her feat, securing all the necessities, including the dark green clothes she'd chosen to help her blend in with the surroundings. She'd wear one of her brunette wigs, so that, not only would she blend in better, but if anyone saw her, she would look less suspicious than a bald woman. A knapsack would hold everything she needed and enable her to climb the fence with her supplies.

The next day, she kept watch from the neighbor's

yard behind his house as he arrived home. As luck would have it, those neighbors were in Hawaii for two weeks, so she didn't have to worry about prying eyes. She'd learned that fact simply by listening to the neighbors call gossip back and forth from yard to yard two days ago. Security around here was a joke with such helpful neighbors around.

Slipping across their lawn, she hiked the fence, hauling herself up and over, suffering just a small scrape on one hand. She paused for a moment to get her bearings, then moved to the first broad shelter tree. A peek through her binoculars proved he hadn't entered the yard yet, so she moved to tree number two and rested there. After a few minutes, she saw the French glass doors swing open. He exited, now dressed in baggy pants and a t-shirt, carrying a few necessary implements in his smooth, pampered hands. He walked to a midway point of the garden, dropped to his knees and began digging in the dirt.

She moved over the outer lawn, her sneakers whispering through the lush, emerald grass. The only other sound was an occasional bird singing or a distant dog barking.

He leaned over to press something. Suddenly the air filled with the melodic sounds of opera. Vivaldi, she thought and smiled. *How convenient*. It was always advantageous to have some noise to cover her actions. She couldn't take a chance on alerting him to her approach.

When she reached the closest tree to the house, she set down her backpack at the base of the trunk, loosening the gather string to reach inside. Thin, latex gloves went on first, then she pulled out the plastic blowpipe. She inserted the dart with care, grateful she had studied the very informative website of a prominent zoo that fully explained how they used this weapon. A little extra practice hadn't hurt, either. Now, she felt like a professional.

Unfortunately for him, he wouldn't be getting a simple animal sedative. A full dose of virulent poison was loaded into the dart. And, if it failed, she had a handgun in her backpack to finish him off.

Once she loaded her rather unusual weapon, she double-checked everything, just to be sure. Preparation complete, she moved into the perfect position that lined her up to face his back.

He hummed to the tune of the music, oblivious. Fidgeting with one plant, he moved to the next. Taking a few calming breaths, she settled.

Cara crouched fifteen feet away. It was essential to get the dart into a large muscle group, so aiming for the haunches would work best. Struggling for patience, she waited as he fiddled and fussed with each damn petal as if it was gold. He finally stood to admire his work.

She blew and heard a *pfft* sound as it left the tube, flying through the air. It landed exactly where she planned. Cursing, he slapped at his hip, looking behind him to find the dart and pluck it out.

But his reaction came too late to save him. The instantaneous injection worked. He looked from his hip, then up at her, his expression confused as he fell to the ground.

As she turned to run, she heard a shriek. Looking up, she saw his wife leaning out of an upstairs window. "Stop," she screamed as Cara sprinted away, looping her knapsack over one wrist as she ran.

She made it to the brick wall and lunged up to gain a hold on the wrought iron bars at the top. Halfway over, she heard a bang and pain ratcheted up her leg. Falling most of the way down on the other side, she got the wind knocked out of her when she hit the ground. Struggling to suck in air, she saw blood on her pants. The crazy old bitch had shot her.

Breath finally returned and she gasped it in, welcoming the blast of air. Ignoring the increasing pain, she forced herself to focus. It would be suicide to head for the parked rental car now the wife had raised an alarm. Scrambling to her feet, she headed, limping, across the neighbors' lawns. She knew what she had to do.

****

Elijah headed home at seven, stopping for dinner at the bar first. He sat in a corner, alone. Tired, he forced himself to eat a decent meal, even if he barely noticed the taste. It didn't help his mood, unfortunately. Before parting, he and Sanchez had decided to have a fresh look at everything they had in the morning and choose a new direction for the investigation. The FBI had been summoned and were expected by late tomorrow afternoon.

He'd just got inside his front door and set his things down when the phone rang and he answered it. "Black."

"Get out here," Sanchez snapped. "Cara's barricaded in her childhood home, asking for you. She's got a gun."

"What the hell happened?"

"No time. Let's go. I'm waiting beside the car."

He grabbed his gun and shield. As he locked the

doors, he spied his partner by the car, huddled against the cold bite of the autumn night. When they were inside the car and he set the GPS, they leapt into gear.

"How did you get here?"

"Ray dropped me off. We were headed home when I got the call. I said I'd get you."

"How did Cara get into the house?" He slapped on sirens and lights.

"The guys on scene said it looks like she picked the locks, but set off the alarm system. The security guys called the local cops, and they phoned us after listening to her demands."

"Did she take any hostages?"

"Luckily, no. Apparently, the owners only live there half the year. They're in Jamaica."

"What does she want?"

"She said she only wants to talk to you. Said she'll only shoot if they try to come in before that happens." Looking at his face, she added, "She's wounded, though. Somebody shot her."

He shouldn't care about the welfare of a killer, but he did. "How bad?"

"Her leg. It's hard to tell. They can see blood on her pants, but she's not saying anything about it."

They raced through the streets for an interminable twenty minutes, siren shrieking, grateful that post rush hour meant lighter traffic. He prayed no one would force the issue on scene. Talking her out safely was his only goal.

When they finally made it to the correct neighborhood, screeching onto the street, they were waved through to join the closest line of cars. Parking near the front of the house, Elijah leapt out with

Sanchez close behind.

He swerved around the other cops, running up to the man clearly in charge of the scene. "Where is she?" he asked, flashing his badge.

The SWAT commander answered. "She's barricaded in the living room and is refusing to talk to anyone except you."

Elijah ignored the grim look of resolve on his face. "Any obvious weapons?"

"She has a semi-automatic pistol on the table in front of her. It's within easy reach."

"She won't use it." He said it with certainty. "It's just a prop to keep everyone else out. It's probably not even loaded."

"You can't possibly know that for sure. Your lieutenant mentioned that you said she was devolving."

"That's true, but she has never hurt anyone who didn't fit the definition of abuser. You don't understand. She would consider shooting one of us a breach of contract."

The commander frowned, obstinacy setting his upper lip in a firm line. "You know we can't trust your best guess on this and possibly put one of our team or the others at risk. Our team is positioned to intervene if it's deemed necessary, and that's my judgement call, not yours."

He had no time to waste arguing. "Do we know how she got wounded?"

"We were just informed that Judge Hart was killed two streets over a while ago. His wife described his assailant, and the description matches your girl. Mrs. Hart shot her as she scaled the wall after the murder."

"Let me go in and talk to her."

He shook his head. "I can't allow that, but we can try over the phone. She gave me the number for you to use." He offered him his cellphone, but Elijah used his own, taking a deep breath, then punching the number in.

"You came." Her voice sounded childlike and teary.

"Of course, I came." He tried to make his voice calm and comforting, despite the frantic activity around him. "I would always come when you ask."

"Will you come and sit with me for a few minutes?"

The commander shook his head.

He lifted his chin, peering toward the window. "Yes. I'm coming in right now. No one else. Just me."

The commander lost the argument when his lieutenant backed him up. At their insistence, he put on a vest. After some debate, they agreed on a thirty-minute pause to see if he could persuade her to come out peacefully. He left his weapons with Sanchez against her protests.

Approaching the house slowly, he raised his voice above the background noise. "Can you see me through the windows, Cara?"

"Yes."

"Okay. I'm coming in now."

Opening the ornate front door, he moved with caution down the elegant hallway and edged into the sitting room. She sat behind a small desk with the pistol laying on the polished surface in front of her. Pointing to a chair placed against the far opposite wall, she said, "Sit there."

"You're hurt. Let me sit next to you."

She shook her head, her lips firm. "No."

Giving up the idea of just overpowering her, he did as she requested, hoping to keep her calm. "Is your leg okay? If you let me, I can stop the bleeding."

"It doesn't matter. I don't even feel it. I don't feel much of anything anymore."

"Did the judge's wife shoot you?"

"Yes." She smiled. "I used a blowpipe to kill him. A unique touch, right?"

"Yes."

"I knew you'd appreciate that. I learned about it on a zoo website." She took a big breath, letting it trickle out. "I went to visit your house."

"I know." He kept his hands in his lap to reassure her. "You should have called me. I could have met you there."

"We both know it's too late for that, Elijah." He saw the lines of exhaustion on her face. His fear for her skyrocketed.

"It's never too late."

"It's kind of sweet you believe that." She cleared her throat. "You really are true blue, aren't you? I keep trying to find a fatal flaw in you, but there aren't any, are there?"

"I'm just a man. I try my best."

She gestured towards the floor, drawing his attention to an Oriental rug. "The first time my father raped me, it was right there on that elegant rug." Staring at it, she seemed transfixed.

He willed away a lump in his throat. "There are no words to tell you how sorry I am for the pain he caused you."

"He turned the stereo up loud and said maybe, if I

was lucky, he'd stop before the album ended."

"Cara, look at me." He was surprised when she followed his request. "Tyler Phelps is dead." Refusing to call that despicable man her father, he continued. "He can't hurt you anymore."

A wistful smile crossed her face. "I wish I could have met you when I was young. I wonder if you would have even looked my way or if you'd have known I'd been tainted."

"I would always see you, Cara. I see you now. We can walk out that door, just the two of us."

She continued as if he hadn't spoken. "I thought I could stop them, you know. I thought if I stopped them all, then no one else would have to endure the pain of being ripped to pieces by them. But there are just too many. If I kill one, five more appear out of whatever dark corner they're spawned in."

"You're so tired, Cara. I'll find you a place where you can rest. I promise."

"Oh, Elijah. You're twenty years too late to save me." She glanced up at the windows, and he read intention on her face.

"Look at me. Let me help you." He lifted his hand to regain her focus.

She smiled, and he caught a glimpse of the woman she could have been. "I chose your face as the last one I wanted to see. You're that rare creature, a truly good man who deserves a wonderful life. Goodbye, Elijah." Standing, she lifted the gun, pointing it towards him and stepping forward into the line of sight.

"No! Cease fire! Cease fire!" He leapt from his chair as bullets pierced the window in a shocking wave of sound. Watching as she crumpled to the floor, he ran, skittering across the shards of glass, to crouch by her side. On the floor, he lifted her into his lap as the SWAT team breached from all directions, the roar of noise overwhelming.

"Cara..." Her eyes registered his presence, then dimmed. He felt her life force creep away.

Sanchez appeared to crouch at his side, checking her pulse. Reaching over, she tugged his arm. "She's gone."

Elijah yanked his arm away, continuing to cradle her. When one of the others asked if he was okay, he simply glared until they left him alone. He continued to ignore them all until the morgue attendants came to carry her away. After they departed, his sole comment to everyone was, "Leave me alone."

Following the vehicle carrying her body to the morgue, he said nothing to Sanchez who remained silent beside him. After their arrival, he stayed alongside the gurney as the attendants checked her into the holding area. Filling out the paperwork saying that her remains should be released to him, he agreed to be responsible for the expense of her burial.

He asked to be alone for a minute. When he finally left the morgue afterwards, he found Sanchez waiting outside. "Let's go get drunk," she said.

"Paperwork."

"The boss gave us the rest of the day off. He said tomorrow's soon enough."

They drank for the rest of the afternoon and all night, saying little, leaving the crowded bar when Ray showed up around midnight. Elijah was vaguely aware of stumbling out and along the street, propped up by his friends on either side. After being shoved into Ray's car, they took him home.

Ray helped him up the steps, then retreated to his car to wait. Inside the brownstone, Sanchez helped him to the couch. "Want to go upstairs to bed?"

"No. This is fine."

"Want us to stay?"

"I'm okay. Don't worry."

He lay down. Shoving a pillow under his head, she left him to go upstairs. He didn't care enough to ask where she was going. After a minute, she returned with a blanket and pulled it over him. "Call me if you need someone to talk to."

"I will." Elijah knew he wouldn't, but it was kind of her to offer. Her steps retreated, then he heard the door click shut behind her. He spent the long, lonely night staring at the ceiling, gulping back embarrassing tears. Around three, he went upstairs to the bathroom and took some painkillers. Stopping and staring through the bedroom doorway at the sheets where she'd lain, he returned downstairs to the couch.

Finally dropping off to sleep, he managed to get two hours of haunted rest before the dawning sun woke him, glaring through the front windows. His pounding head made a joke of his preventative dose of drugs. Nausea threatened. For the first time in his life, he wished he had access to sleeping medication, just enough to check out for a week or two. His only prevailing thought was that he'd failed her, winning a few battles, but losing the long, bitter war.

This time, he couldn't help feeling that the bad guys had won once again.

Sanchez showed up at eight a.m., banging on the front door until he answered. He refused to go to work

with her. "What do I tell the boss?" she asked, concern showing in the lines of her face.

"I don't care." He crawled back onto the couch, turning his back. After she left, he fell into an exhausted slumber, nightmares refusing to let him rest. When he woke again around noon, Sanchez sat curled in the upholstered armchair next to him, a magazine sitting in her lap.

His dry mouth tasted like parchment paper. He sat up, rubbing his eyes. "What the hell are you doing here?"

"Dumb question. You're my partner, aren't you?"

"How did you get in? I locked the door after you left."

"I took your keys." She handed him a glass of cool water that had been sitting on the coffee table and he forced himself to take a sip. "Feel any better?"

He ran a hand through his unruly hair. "Well, the hammer's gone from my head, mostly anyway. I need to get something to eat, though."

"Wheat toast with a little butter?"

"Yeah. Thanks, Mom."

Snorting a laugh, she went to fetch it for him. After a few minutes of rustling around, she returned, handing him the plate and watching while he forced himself to eat it. He managed to gag it down. Pushing away the empty plate, he asked, "What'd the boss have to say?"

"Good job, blah blah, come and see him when you get in."

He winced, looking down at his rumpled clothes. "Guess I better go and have a shower."

She sniffed, her eyes bugging out theatrically. "Yeah, good idea. We all need a little fresh air at this point. It'd probably be okay with him if you went in tomorrow if you need more time."

"No. Thanks. Putting it off won't change anything." After he cleaned up and dressed, they walked over together, not bothering to hurry.

Tapping his arm to reassure him, she said, "You did the best you could."

"It wasn't enough. Everybody in her life let her down, me included."

"She was already past the point of saving when you met her."

"Maybe. Maybe not. I guess we'll never know now."

They arrived at the precinct, and he ignored the curious looks from his co-workers. When he reported to his lieutenant's office, the commissioner was waiting. The two men thanked him for solving the case and the commissioner left. His lieutenant mentioned a press briefing later.

"I'm sorry, sir. Perhaps Sanchez could take care of it this time. I would like to take some personal leave immediately after I file my report."

His boss looked at him, somber-eyed. "Of course. Take all the time you need."

He nodded. "Thank you, sir."

Leaning against his desk, he sighed. "One thing to consider, Elijah, while you're taking some time for reflection. You couldn't have saved her. She knew she would have, at the very least, been locked up in a cage for eternity. There is, perhaps, some small kindness in being able to choose your own way out."

He was lucky his boss gave a damn. Not all of them did. Nodding, he thanked him and left.

A few hours later, after he'd filed the report and his paperwork for days off, Sanchez walked him home again. As he let himself in the door, she said, "Let me know when you're going to have the burial. I'd like to be there."

Blowing air out through his teeth, he said, "Thanks. I'll call you in a few days."

He drank his way through the next few days, not proud of it, but needing something to blot out the pain. On the fourth day, her body was released. Not surprisingly, no one had fought him for the privilege of burying her. Saturday morning, he and Sanchez stood at the cemetery closest to his house, watching the grave attendants lower her casket into the ground as the dark, gray day drizzled onto their bare heads. "What are you gonna put on the headstone? Just her name and the date?"

Reaching into his pocket, he withdrew the note she'd had tucked into her clothes. After reading it, Sanchez looked up at him, puzzled. "Who's this from?"

"Dr. Hayes found it inside her blouse. It was the only thing she took from my house."

"I wonder why."

He sighed. "I think she was under the impression it must be something highly personal to me. The truth is, I found it in an old book I bought at auction and thought it was special, so I just tucked it away. How many of us will ever be loved like that?"

"You're a romantic, my friend."

"She deserves something more than her name to mark her place."

As the attendants began to shovel loose dirt over her coffin, he went forward, threw in a single rose, then turned and walked away.

Epilogue

A week later, Elijah was doing his backlog of laundry in preparation for going back to work when a doorbell sounded at his front door. He answered it to find an older man in a pristine business suit waiting.

"Detective Black?"

"Yes."

"My name is Aaron Stills."

The name rang a faint bell in his memory, but his brain was too muddled to place it.

"I'm Cara Belton's attorney. We spoke on the phone not long ago."

The memory flooded back. "Oh, yes, Mr. Stills. I remember now. How can I help you?"

"May I come in for a moment?"

"Certainly." Standing back to let the other man enter, he offered him a seat in the living room which he took. He sat in the opposite chair. "What brings you to my neighborhood?"

"Ms. Belton asked me to give you several things after her death." He grimaced. "I didn't, of course, realize her plans at the time of our discussion."

"When did she come to see you?"

"Two days before she…died. I was quite surprised to see her after all these years." He fiddled with his jacket. "Were you aware that she drew up a will naming you as the sole beneficiary of her estate?"

It stole his breath. "No. Why on earth would she do such a thing?"

He pulled an envelope from his leather briefcase and handed it to him. "She said this would explain things." Clearing his throat, he continued. "At any rate, the estate is currently worth approximately eight million dollars. It will, of course, have to go through probate, which will take some time. I will start the proceedings immediately and keep you informed of the progress. There are no remaining family members, so it should be quite straightforward."

She had surprised him once again. He felt compelled to ask one last question. "How did she seem when you met with her?"

He paused to consider the question. "She seemed calm and quite resolute. I realized, afterward, that she had made her decision and was at peace with it."

Elijah thought about the lawyer's words after he left.

Calm.

Resolute.

It made things a little easier, somehow.

He steeled himself to open the letter. What more could there be for her to say? Picking up the letter opener, he slit the envelope, and noticed the faint aroma of her perfume wafting out. The note inside was handwritten.

Dear Elijah,

If you are reading this, I have finished my journey to what I hope is a better world. I want you to know that this mess is not your fault. You were never meant to save me, but to be a witness to both my life and death, to my story as a whole.

Being part of the wind that swirls around your face every day is much better than being stuck in a cage.

And now, to business. I left you my money for two reasons: to enjoy and to find a way to help other children who have suffered the abuse I did. I put all my trust in your ability to discern which avenues would help the most victims.

I'd say a 50/50 split would be a fair distribution. That way, you can have what you need and enjoy in life without worrying about it and still be able to administer the other half of the money to appropriate projects for my cause.

I can't imagine more trusted hands in which to leave this bequest.

And so, goodbye, my one true friend.

I'll hold you in my heart

Forever,

Cara

He read the note over, several times, imagining her writing it. In the end, he carried her final message up and placed it in the same drawer in which he used to keep the other letter, by itself, for his eyes only.

Coming Soon:

Dark Motives: The Elijah Black Trilogy, Book 2:

Chapter One

Detective Alvia Sanchez waited in the car, as she often did on Friday mornings, for Elijah to place his rose on Cara's grave and return.

The irreverent side of her wanted to tell him the weekly visits were overkill, but she kept her mouth zipped. Each to his own. She would never understand his connection to a serial killer. At least her partner had returned from the depths of despair, even though he wasn't yet powering at full throttle.

He finally returned, folding his long legs and climbing behind the wheel. She paused as he started the car, then handed him a donut. Shrugging, he ate it as he wound his way through the endless lines of gravestones to the ornate, black iron front gate. It was a sign of the times that his usual healthy food choices had taken a temporary back seat to her far less prudent offerings.

After arriving at their precinct, they were hailed at the top of the stairs by Detective Albert Jones. Brown-haired, brown-eyed and remarkably average in every way, he never stood out, but was, at least, reliable. Even his shirt was a bland beige, as though color had abandoned the cause. "Boss wants to see you both pronto," he said, a smirk twisting his pale face.

Thanking him, they diverted down the long hall to Lieutenant Allen Porter's office. He looked distracted, as always. With the day barely begun, his restless hands had already disturbed his graying hair. "Sit down," he said, gesturing at the timeworn chairs across the desk from his own. "We just caught a murder uptown. Sylvia Bennett, owner of a string of five-star restaurants, was found shot to death in her apartment. She's a socialite, very high profile, plastered all over social media. I need you two to handle this one."

"Yes, sir," Elijah said. "Are there other detectives on scene?"

"Hadley and Davis are holding it for you. They're overseeing the evidence team and managing crowd control. Someone from the medical examiner's office should have arrived by the time you get there. They're still short-handed."

Elijah knew Hadley in particular wouldn't be happy at him and Sanchez taking point on this case or any other. He typically made being unsatisfied a full-time occupation. "Anything else, sir?"

Their boss gave a pronounced sigh. "I hope I'm wrong, but from what I've been told, it feels like a symbolic killing which might mean the killer's not done. Make my workday easier by proving me wrong." He pushed a square of colored paper with the address scrawled on it across the desk. "Keep me informed."

"Yes, sir."

They fought their way through what remained of the morning's rush hour traffic to an elegant high rise uptown. A sizable crowd had already gathered outside, undeterred by the cool autumn air. New York news hounds were a ravenous bunch, chomping on the fetid meat of murder. Leaving their car parked near the entrance brought a scowl to the stalwart doorman's face until they held up their credentials. He nodded and waved them inside, holding back the group of milling reporters who shoved too close to the door. Their shouted questions sounded muffled from the interior.

"Tenth floor," Elijah said to Sanchez, nodding at the cop stationed in the downstairs hall as they walked past. Entering the elevator, they waited as the gleaming doors closed and the snug metal box lifted them upwards. On their arrival, they counted six spacious apartments on the floor, three on each side. The only thing that bought you so much square footage in this city was a veritable hoard of money. They headed for the one unit in the far corner. Sounds of activity beckoned them through the open door into the carnage beyond.

Detective Barry "Bear" Davis looked up and nodded a greeting, his smile reaching his expressive blue eyes. He'd once been a champion linebacker in university until a knee injury forced him out of a promising future in football. His sheer brawn was enough to intimidate most criminals. A pleasant, easygoing guy, he was well-liked by everyone, especially the ladies who were drawn to both his broad shoulders and his thick, golden hair.

His partner, Phil Hadley, was another story. He saw them coming and crossed his arms, a familiar, snarky expression compressing his face. Considered a snappy dresser, at least by himself, his mud-colored hair was coiffed so that his bangs lifted off his thin, pinched forehead.

Davis moved beside Elijah, knowing he and Hadley didn't get along. "Hey, you two. We've got a forty-two-year-old female, Sylvia Bennett, dead from three bullet wounds. Doc's with her now, so we should have time of death in a minute."

"No witnesses?"

"Two of the guys just started canvassing the neighbors. Haven't heard anything yet."

"Who found her?"

"The housekeeper." He pointed through a doorway to the nearby bedroom where a small, dark-haired woman sat in a chair, sobbing. Framed by the opening, she appeared as if posed for a painting titled Sorrow, her tear-stained face the very definition of melancholy.

"Can you take care of her?" he asked Sanchez. Nodding, she moved over to the other woman and crouched down beside her. Clasping one of her hands, she began speaking softly in Spanish. For all of her brashness, she had an uncanny way with witnesses that was invaluable.

Elijah always proved more adept with the presentation of the crime itself and the picture the killer left behind. He wished they had been the first ones to arrive on scene. First impressions, unsullied by the presence of others, were always helpful. Starting towards the body, he was thwarted by Hadley stepping in front of him, his legs braced and his hands dangling at each side, curled into fists. "Busy grabbing everyone's cases these days, aren't you, boy wonder? Wouldn't want anyone else smeared all over the front page."

His jaw set, he met the other man's accusing gaze. Territorial issues caused by an overblown ego wasted valuable time better spent on investigation. "I go wherever my lieutenant requires me to assist. If you have a problem with that, I suggest you take your complaints up with him."

Swearing under his breath, the other man stormed off, stomping his feet like a rebellious toddler. His renowned temper would get him fired one day, but it hadn't happened yet. Davis shrugged, waved goodbye and followed Hadley out the door. It was a good thing Davis could put up with his partner because no one else seemed interested in such an exhausting job.

Elijah approached Dr. Stanford Hayes as the medical examiner straightened. "Good morning, doc. I thought your assistant would be here."

"Which assistant? The latest one just quit. Not many can stand up to the workload." The tall, gray-haired man tightened his lips to a flat line. "Your lieutenant asked me to take a look because of the specific nature of the injuries." He gestured towards the body and stood aside so Elijah could take a gander.

One glance told the story and had him cringing. The oozing wounds were in each of the woman's breasts and in between her legs, the blood an indelible red marker on her clothes. "I see what you mean. It's a statement of sorts as if he's attacking women in general. That makes me worry she won't be the last."

A word about the author...

Dianne McCartney has been writing for seventeen years and has won sixty-three writing awards in contests across Texas and Oklahoma. She is a long-standing member of the Oklahoma Writers Federation, Inc. and a proud member of the Rose Rock Writers.

http://www.diannemccartney.com
Twitter: @AuthorDMcC
Instagram: diannemccartney1200
Facebook:
https://www.facebook.com/dianne.mccartney.3914

www.ingramcontent.com/pod-product-compliance
Lightning Source LLC
Chambersburg PA
CBHW070117260626
47160CB00004B/1515